Diane stepped closer until her chest pressed gently against his. Hale slid his arms around her, pulling her closer still and cupping her backside. Diane's mouth opened and she uttered a weak moan. She put her arms around his neck, lifting her lips blindly to find his kiss.

It was just what she needed then, hot and deep and all consuming. Their lips worked together with a deliberate slowness that left her dizzy and disoriented. Hips touching, they were separated only by her bikini briefs. Together their breathing melded and hissed like a whisper in their ears with a growing urgency. The prelude was rich with promise, and they took their time to enjoy each movement and touch. The intensity was building until they both felt it in the rush of blood through their veins, the throbbing in their groins that edged toward release.

Suddenly Hale pulled his mouth free, momentarily teasing her lips with the tip of his tongue. Her breasts were so tender and sensitive they ached.

"Do it again," she pleaded.

Books by Sandra Kitt

Kimani Romance

*RSVP with Love
Promises in Paradise

*Hollington Homecoming

SANDRA KITT

is the author of almost forty published novels and novellas. Her work has been cited by Amazon.com and *Library Journal* among their Best Contemporary Novels of the Year for several years. She has been nominated for the NAACP Image Award in Fiction, and received a Waldenbooks award, a Lifetime Achievement award from *RT Book Reviews* and the 2002 Service Award from RWA. Sandra is the first African American writer to ever publish with Harlequin Books.

A onetime graphic designer and illustrator, Sandra has designed cards for UNICEF and illustrated books for the late science writer Isaac Asimov. A former information specialist in astronomy and astrophysics at the American Museum of Natural History, she recently worked for three months at the European Southern Observatory in Munich.

Sandra has been a guest speaker at NYU, Penn State, Sarah Lawrence and Columbia University. She serves on the Advisory Board of St. Jude Children's Research Hospital in Memphis, Tennessee. *For All We Know,* a romance novel released in 2008, was written to benefit St. Jude. Sandra lives in New York City.

Promises
in
Paradise

Sandra Kitt

KIMANI
ROMANCE

KIMANI PRESS™

ISBN-13: 978-0-373-86169-9

Recycling programs
for this product may
not exist in your area.

PROMISES IN PARADISE

www.kimanipress.com

Printed in U.S.A.

Dear Reader,

I cannot think of a more romantic setting for a story than an island in the Caribbean. For those of you who have visited many of the islands as I have, you know what I'm talking about! The pure aquamarine sea and serene white-sand beaches alone are worth the price of admission.

My favorite island has always been St. John, one of the three U.S. Virgin Islands. I've returned there dozens of times. Not only that, but some of my most memorable (and romantic) vacations have taken place there, so it was an obvious choice as a rendezvous point for my hero and heroine in *Promises in Paradise*.

I hope you are swept away by the magic of St. John and the thrill of the love and romance in Diane and Hale's story.

Take care,

Sandra Kitt

Chapter 1

Uttering an obligatory thank-you and grabbing the claim ticket from the valet, Diane Maxwell took a deep breath and began to hurry down the street toward the minimalist and very modern entrance of the Maryland Museum of African American Culture in Baltimore. She knew the title was much longer than that, but she didn't have time for formality...or to remember.

Instead, she concentrated on not twisting her ankle in her three-inch dress sandals, or getting the heel caught in the hem of her gown.

It was *cold*. Much colder than Diane wanted to accept, even though it was the second week of December. She was dismayed and annoyed that her breath expelled in a chilly vapor. Yet she would not admit to the vanity and poor judgment that had her out for the evening with nothing warmer than a cashmere shawl wrapped artfully around her shoulders, and no panty hose.

She'd reasoned that she was only going from her car to the entrance of the museum, but she hadn't counted on the valet stand being a city block away. She was already *beyond* late for the gala function being held at the beautiful facility, but her running-walk had more to do with the goose bumps rising on her exposed arms.

Diane slowed her pace and stopped in front of the museum entrance, covertly straightening the bodice of her gown. She tucked her evening clutch under her elbow and quickly shook out the yards of silk that made up the skirt. She squared her shoulders and tried to give the appearance of a woman of poise and presence and not the tomboy hoyden she was once known as. But there was no audience for her little pretense or her grand entrance.

Once inside the glass doors she was immediately assailed by the warmth and met with the hum of conversation from an upper level of the museum.

"Good evening. Thank you for coming tonight."

Diane turned to the voice to her left, where a reception table had been set up. Behind it sat a lone woman, her folded hands atop a spreadsheet of the names of guests attending the function. She smiled a greeting in return and approached the table. The matron was attired in an overly bright red dress, with a rhinestone pendant necklace lost in the cleavage of her bosom.

"May I have your name, please?" the woman asked, her fingertip poised to run down the list.

"Maxwell. Dr. Diane. I'm here in place of my father, Adam Maxwell."

"Maxwell…Max…yes, here it is. Oh, he's one of the special guests tonight." She placed a check next to the name.

Diane glanced quickly around the empty entrance.

"Am I very late?" she asked, accepting the card calligraphed with her father's name and a table number.

"You're the last to arrive. They just started serving dinner, but you know how the folks are," the woman said with a knowing smile. "The reception ended late 'cause they couldn't get people to stop drinking and talking."

Even as she explained Diane could hear one voice over a microphone introducing herself and welcoming everyone to the annual dinner.

"You better hurry." The woman chuckled. "It's embarrassing to walk in when someone is talking."

"You're right." Diane grinned sheepishly.

She lifted the skirt of her gown and, graceful and athletic, took the stairs two at a time, stiletto heels, rustling silk and all.

"Be careful!" the woman whispered loudly behind her.

At the top of the stairs Diane regained her composure, dropping the skirt and again shaking out the fabric. She looked inside a large darkened room that had been set up with some twenty tables, each capable of seating ten people. She wasn't paying much attention to the speaker, an elegantly dressed woman about her own age, making opening remarks about the event. Instead, Diane was aware that it wasn't going to be that easy to find her table now that the lights had been dimmed. But she took heart in the fact that the first course was being served so no one would be any wiser to her late appearance.

"Can I help you?"

Diane turned to another voice and this time found a young man waiting to assist her. He held out his hand and she realized he wanted her table card. After briefly scanning it he pointed to a table across the room.

Diane sighed. The table was, unfortunately, among those right in front of a raised dais. She gave the young man a charming smile.

"You know, it's not that important for me to sit there, is it? I'm sure I can find a seat somewhere else. Maybe near the back..."

"I'll escort the lady to her seat."

Diane whipped around to find a tall man calmly regarding her. In an instant three things became apparent to her. He was superbly outfitted in a tuxedo that did justice to his shoulders and to a certain haughtiness in his features. She knew who he was. And she wasn't happy to see him.

There was a fourth thing, but Diane purposefully ignored its manifestations. It caused a sudden flutter in her stomach and a dry mouth. But again, instantly, she returned to her first observation. The tux forced her to fast-forward her memories and impressions of Hale Cameron from rough, street-smart and sullen to this sudden real-time urbane and sophisticated presence. The unexpected time warp was startling.

"Oh. It's you."

"Diane," he acknowledged.

She stared, caught off guard. He said her name with both surprise and familiarity. It was that second recognition that caused Diane to change, her eyes hardening and her mouth grimacing in annoyance.

"Fancy running into you," he drawled, his gaze never leaving her face.

Diane quickly experienced a very unwelcome sense of exposure and vulnerability, as if he'd hit a nerve. Deliberately or not. She didn't like her reaction at all.

"This certainly is the last place I expected to see you, Hale," she said, staring him down.

He raised his brows but didn't take the bait.

"I knew your father was on the list tonight. I was looking forward to seeing him. Sorry he couldn't make it."

Diane knew he was fishing for more information but she was not about to be chatty and pleasant to him.

"Something came up."

"I believe you," Hale said smoothly. "Adam would have gotten here on time, and wouldn't slink in late."

Her sharp retort died on her tongue. There was suddenly applause in the room beyond, bringing her back to the present. Diane pulled herself together, but only to turn her back on Hale as he watched her, his expression amused.

"I'll find my own seat," she said firmly to the assistant at the door. She turned back to Hale and gave him a frosty stare. "Yes, I'm late but it was unavoidable. My father will understand."

"I'm sure you count on that." He nodded, taking a large gulp of wine from a glass he'd been holding down at his side.

Hale then summarily handed the empty glass to the assistant, who had stood silently listening to the verbal sparring.

"I'll escort her to her seat," Hale said again.

"Look, I don't want—"

Diane stopped abruptly rather than create a scene when an elderly couple appeared out of the darkened dinner hall, obviously about to leave. Spotting Hale, their faces lit with warm smiles, they called and reached out to him. The woman offered an overly rouged cheek and the man, probably her husband, took Hale's hand to shake.

"Sorry we have to leave, Hale. Getting too old for

these late nights," the man said in a tired, gravelly voice.

"We certainly weren't going to leave before having that very expensive dinner we paid for," the wife said with false indignation.

They all laughed as Diane stood and witnessed the exchange. In a way she was fascinated by the affection that the older couple obviously held for Hale and that he seemed to have for them. In all fairness, she recalled that this was the way Hale had always been toward her father, Adam. And her father toward him. Holding Hale in high regard. Talking about him and praising him... ad nauseam.

She tried to move quietly away but only succeeded in drawing the couple's attention.

"Mr. and Mrs. Hightower, this is Diane Maxwell," Hale finally introduced her.

Again there was applause from the room and some laughter. Diane tried to ignore it and smiled graciously at the couple regarding her with mild curiosity.

"Dr. Maxwell," she clarified, more for Hale's sake than the older couple. "It's nice to meet you but don't let me interrupt. I see you're leaving, and I really need to go in..."

"You're Adam's daughter. I've heard so much about you," Mrs. Hightower cut in, beaming at her. "From Adam, of course. We were so hoping to see him tonight."

"He knows how to work a room," Hale commented.

Mr. Hightower chuckled. "He sure can. He also knows how to separate folks from their money for one cause or another."

Diane, faced with such adoration, smiled wanly. "I know I'm a poor substitute..."

"Oh, not at all, young lady. You're a very pretty one," Mr. Hightower said.

"I'll let my father know he was missed."

She stood aside then, as goodbyes were now shared between Hale and the couple and they made their way to the elevator to leave. Diane did not wait for their final departure, but turned to the gala room in hopes of finally slipping into a vacant place at any of the tables near the entrance. She knew that it was inevitable that some people did not make it to these events and there were a number of empty seats.

Before she could reach a nearby table, let alone greet the occupants and apologize for arriving late, someone placed a hand at the small of her back and was firmly guiding her along between the tables and toward the front of the room. Nonplussed, Diane glanced over her shoulder and found Hale close behind her. They were halfway into the room. To stop and object now to his interference would have caused a commotion and embarrassment. Diane, seething with helplessness, had no choice but to allow herself to be directed.

When they reached her table, Hale pulled out her chair, holding it until she sat down. She smiled a greeting to those who glanced her way as she whispered her apologies. She settled herself, actually glad that the minor ordeal was over. She looked over her shoulder in time to see Hale take a seat several tables away.

She was very curious to know why he was even there.

Unlike the occupants of her table, who were much older and the vanguards of another generation of philanthropists, Hale's table was filled with men and

women his own age. The four or five women were all
attractive, beautifully dressed and seemed to have a lot
to say to him, vying for his attention…which, Diane
noticed, he didn't deny them. The men also seemed to
hang on his every word, with respect and interest and
easy camaraderie.

Diane made a little sniff of indifference and turned
to answer the waiter who wanted to know if she desired
red or white wine with her dinner.

Thankfully, she considered, being late had spared her
the need to listen through most of the program, leaving
only award presentations and acceptance remarks. One
of those awards was for her father.

When the announcement was made for the Joshua J.
Abernathy Humanist Award for excellence in education,
Diane stood to make her way to the stage. As she did so,
hoping not to trip over audio cables or someone's feet,
the evening's MC expressed relief that she had finally
arrived, fearing that the one seat at the reserved table
would remain empty and the award mailed in absentia
to its recipient. Mild laughter followed these comments
as Diane reached the podium. Allowing the applause
to die away she realized, looking out over the audience
who were all staring at her, she'd never prepared any
remarks.

"Actually," Diane began after she'd accepted the
Revere Bowl and the envelope containing the award
check and posed for a quick photo with the museum
president, "I got lost."

Her honest and guileless opening received genuine
laughter. She stood looking lovely and unflustered and
pleased with herself for having charmed them.

Take that, Diane said to herself, knowing Hale was

in the audience watching. Probably hoping that she'd mess up.

"My father always says I am directionally challenged, but a great swimmer and generally acceptable as a daughter. So, I'm forgiven my few shortcomings."

There was more laughter from the audience and she relaxed, thinking quickly on her feet. She would be brief and succinct and do Adam Maxwell proud.

"My father sends his regrets at not being here tonight. There was an unavoidable conflict. It's my pleasure and honor to be here in his place. As you know Adam Maxwell has always been supportive of Into the Future programs and the great work you do in furthering the opportunities for black youngsters to pursue education and their dreams. He's very moved to be recognized with this award for his work, but says he doesn't deserve it. I agree."

There were some chuckles, but it was obvious that the audience was taken aback by this pronouncement.

"My father would be the first to waive the praise and say he's only doing what desperately needs to be done. Along the way in his life and career there were people to guide and support him, believe in him. He feels he's simply returning the favor. Paying it forward, so to speak.

"Nonetheless I am most humbled, and very happy to accept on his behalf your appreciation of his work and contribution. Also on my father's behalf, I will be donating the monetary award to your organization to be used to further your mission. Encouraging black students who might otherwise have limited opportunities for a productive and happy future."

The audience came to their feet and showed their surprise and approval with enthusiastic sustained applause. Diane stood regal and still, glancing out over the guests with a genuine smile.

"Thank you, from my father and from myself. Again, I apologize for my late arrival but I wouldn't have missed tonight for anything."

She turned and left the stage, stopping only briefly to accept thanks from the director of Into the Future for the gift of her father's award check. The applause continued until she took her seat.

As she did so Diane hazarded a glance over her shoulder to Hale's table. Everyone around him had taken their seats but he was still standing and applauding until the end, his expression indiscernible in the dimly lit room. She hoped she achieved total indifference to his response as she sat down again. But she knew Hale's gaze followed her.

The presentations continued. Diane found that as she was being served her dinner everyone else had pretty much finished. She covertly ate enough of the duck confit and asparagus, artfully tied with a strip of red pepper, to quell her growling stomach before she allowed her plate to be removed. She slowly sipped her wine, giving her something to do as conversation happened around her. She was steadfast in her resolve to ignore the quiet but constant buzz of talk and laughter coming from Hale's table.

She focused her attention on the stage and podium, to others receiving awards and giving thanks. Having performed as she'd been required to, Diane realized she was also no longer the subject of admiring glances, appreciative smiles or even mild curiosity. She felt suddenly, oddly, out of sync with the evening and everyone around her. And alone, as if she didn't belong.

Inexplicably, she blamed Hale Cameron for her feelings.

As the dessert was being served, Diane picked up her fork and carefully broke off some of the tiramisu but she couldn't really enjoy it. She was suddenly acutely aware of Hale and his presence in the room, and his relationship to her father. And how her acceptance remarks, off-the-cuff and sincere and totally inadvertent, had been a lot about him.

Seeing him at the entrance to the gala room had stunned her and caught her completely off guard. The tall, self-possessed, rather good-looking man in formal attire had confused her. Seeing him so suddenly, so unexpectedly, had disturbed history and rattled her expectations. She didn't know what to make of this person, this apparition who seemed to have morphed from her memories into a different being.

Suddenly the man seated to her left, unaware, knocked her evening clutch off the table as he shifted in his chair. Diane quickly bent to retrieve it and took yet another opportunity to check out the table behind her and to the right. Hale had his arm resting along the top of the chair of a woman next to him as he leaned close to hear what she was saying. The woman, petite and—as much as Diane hated to admit it—adorable, had her lips very close to Hale's ear and his undivided attention. Diane faced forward once more, placing her bag in her lap. She pushed her dessert plate away.

The evening was beginning to seem endless.

It had certainly never occurred to Diane that she would ever seen Hale Cameron again, let alone at this kind of evening that had brought out many of D.C.'s black education elite. It had been…what…more than ten years since they'd spoken to one another. Yet his name

and the evolution of his life had been an indelible part
of her own, thanks to her father.

Diane knew that she and Hale lived in the same city,
D.C., but didn't move in the same circles. She'd worked
hard to make sure their paths would never cross. But
even if she'd wanted to never see or hear the name Hale
Cameron again in her lifetime, the chances were slim
to none.

In all honesty, Diane considered dispiritedly, as
laughter rang out from Hale's table, it would not have
been because of her father's liking for the younger man
but all because of her own steadfast lack of it.

Hale covertly checked his watch and stole a quick
glance at the printed program in front of him. Two more
awards and then it will all be over.

He tried to roll his shoulders back to ease the tightness
across the top. He crossed his legs as he lounged back
in his chair, his tux jacket unbuttoned. He looked to
the temporary stage as the next presentation was made,
but out of his peripheral vision there was no avoiding
a full-on view of Diane as she sat listening to the
proceedings. Elegant. Queenly. Beautiful. Bitch.

Hale hurriedly uncrossed his legs and sat up straight.
His jaw tensed with the sway of his thoughts.

That was totally uncool, he told himself in
irritation.

His glance strayed in her direction again. It had been
a long time. Years and years, and then some. And yet,
he was genuinely stunned by the difference between
then and now, at least physically, as he tried to adjust
his thinking, his memories, to fit the moment.

He mentally shook his head. In another way he was
also sure that nothing had changed. At least, between

the two of them. From Diane's very cold attitude to her biting comments, he might just as well have been dead to her.

Hale considered their peculiar history and the awkward melding of their lives. He knew everything about Diane Maxwell. Far more than she'd appreciate his knowing, more than was comfortable from his point of view. All of which, however, had only served to keep them connected over the years, like an invisible umbilical or Bungee cord.

The woman seated next to him shifted slowly in her chair and sighed. Hale immediately bent toward her.

"Everything okay?"

She nodded, taking a tiny sip of water. "I'm getting a little tired."

"We can leave now if you want." He placed his napkin on the table and began pushing his chair back. She touched his arm.

"No, not yet. It's almost over, Hale. I can wait."

"Are you sure?"

She smiled at him in the darkened room. "Believe me, if I wasn't, you'd be the second person to know." She patted his arm, and gave her attention back to the front of the room.

Satisfied, Hale relaxed. His gaze wandered back to Diane.

She'd cut her hair.

He remembered a wild mane of thick but loosely textured natural hair that he used to call her Diana Ross wannabe look. She'd hated his teasing, thinking herself far more original. In truth, Hale had to admit that Diane had never really been the kind of girl who fussed over her looks or worried about her hair. Especially since she was a swimmer. Long ago it was more that she was comfortable with her own natural appeal and never felt the need to play on it, and it didn't need improvements. Studying her now, it was obvious that had changed.

The woman she'd become was…he couldn't even say it. He couldn't find the right words because they would be so foreign to what Diane used to be and what he'd known of her. The girl was gone. The fearless, but awkward and innocent teenager had been replaced in a major way. Hale may not have been able to get his memories straight around it, but his present state of mind was another matter.

Uncomfortable with having been forced back into the past, he was anxious for the evening to be over.

Even as the applause started on the closing remarks of the hostess and MC, people were getting up, saying good-night to one another and heading with purpose for the exit. Hale quickly stood, offering a hand to his companion as she slowly rose from her chair. Hale offered his arm. She held on as they left the room. There was a crowd of people around the elevator, but many others were filing down the staircase in a wave of black tuxedos and colorful dresses.

"Hale, I'll just be a minute."

"I'll wait here," he said, releasing her hand and watching her closely as she headed toward the ladies' room.

The room was almost empty by the time Diane was finally able to leave. Even then she was accompanied by one of her father's professional friends, who was asking her to have Adam call him. It had been a long time since they'd gotten together and they were overdue.

Diane smiled graciously. "I certainly will give him

your message. He loves the whole let's-do-lunch thing
but he's terrible about making it happen."

"I know," the elderly man lamented. "Adam never
did suffer the details very well. I've always enjoyed our
conversations. Give him my best."

"I will. Get home safe," Diane said and the gentleman,
alone, walked away.

She waited just a moment longer before leaving
the room, her father's Revere Bowl in her hands. She
looked up and saw Hale. He was standing alone, his gaze
focused absently on the last group of guests descending
the staircase. For just a moment Diane quietly watched
him, accepting that she no longer recognized the young
man she used to know. In that moment she was very
curious about this new person, this grown man. What
was he doing here? How had he become involved with
such an influential and select group of professional
folks?

Was the tux rented?

As curious as Diane suddenly was about Hale, she
accepted that it would be a snowy day in hell before she
asked her father for details.

Undetected, she walked away from him to make one
more stop before her drive home.

In the ladies' room, one woman was washing her
hands. The second, a small, lovely young woman, was
sitting in the outer lounge area reapplying lipstick. Diane
recognized her as Hale's dinner companion. The woman
caught her gaze briefly in the mirror and offered a faint
but friendly smile. Diane automatically responded in
passing.

When she finished and was ready to leave it was
in time to see Hale and the woman about to board the

elevator. Diane made the decision to walk down, but was spotted by the woman, who waved at her.

"You're just in time. We'll hold the door."

Unable to come up with a reason why she shouldn't ride with them, Diane hurried to the elevator and entered.

She avoided looking at Hale. "Thanks."

The word caught in her throat. She sounded breathless to her own ears. Not because she was in a closed, confined place with Hale, but because she was suddenly aware that his companion was very pregnant.

The other woman was saying something. Introducing herself. Jenna. Stunned, Diane couldn't hear properly. She had to force herself to focus, to clear her head and lift her gaze to the other woman.

"...about your father. He sounds like a wonderful man," the woman said.

Diane nodded absently, trying to think.

Think!

"Ah...yes. Thank you. I agree but I'm biased. He's far from perfect, but if I don't agree, I'll probably sound mean-spirited."

"Which is it?" Hale asked.

Diane's eyes sparked but she did her best to hide it. She looked at Hale, her gaze steady. "I'm lucky that he's my father. He's probably a better person than I am."

A muscle in Hale's jaw tightened and his dark eyes took her in, steady...and unforgiving.

"I don't believe that," Jenna demurred. "Your speech was so warm and loving. I'd say, like father, like daughter. Right, Hale?"

It was too long a moment before he responded and Diane braced herself for something sly and cutting.

"I think that's fair," he murmured.

The elevator eased to a stop and the doors opened. The entrance lobby was almost deserted, except for night staff, the director and several others who, once again surrounding Diane, congratulated her father and asked that he be thanked for so generously donating his award check to the cause.

Before Diane could finally bid Hale and Jenna goodnight, Hale's voice halted her.

"Is your car in the museum lot?"

Diane looked puzzled. "Yes. Why did you ask?"

"So's mine. If you follow me I'll lead you back to 295. That will take you right to the Belt. You'll find your way home from there."

"I'll be fine. You don't have to…"

"Do you leave the lot and go to your right or left? The highway entrance is a quarter of a mile east of here."

Diane stared blankly at him. Jenna laughed. "I think it's a man thing. I couldn't tell you if we're east or west, either. Come on. It's not going to take us out of the way."

Diane wanted to protest again but she knew she'd only come off as ungrateful and stubborn. She glanced covertly at Hale only to find him regarding Jenna affectionately.

Okay. So she's pregnant, pretty and nice.

"Thanks," Diane murmured, quietly giving in.

Diane watched Hale help Jenna with her winter coat that, when buttoned, ballooned over her protruding belly. She found it humiliating to trail several feet behind Hale and Jenna as, her hand looped through his bent arm, he slowly walked them all back to the parking lot. Diane tried to control her shivers, the rush of frosty air biting into her skin and penetrating deep to her bones. To add insult to injury, her nose was starting to run. She began sniffling.

If Jenna or Hale noticed they gave no indication. The pace continued leisurely for Jenna's sake, and Diane gritted her teeth, her eyes now watering from the cold, until they reached the lot. Her car was brought out first. She gave the attendant a very large tip for having turned on her heater full blast. She fell into the seat, closing the door with a deep sigh of relief.

She waited for the same service for Hale and Jenna, watching them both through her windshield. Not so much Jenna but Hale.

Patience, consideration, kindness and tenderness were not words she would ever have associated with him. At least not the Hale she used to know. But Diane was taken aback, almost mesmerized, by his attention to Jenna. She didn't know what to think, what to feel. Their whole encounter that evening had so been outside their history that she felt as if she'd stepped back to the year she was seventeen. That's where she and Hale Cameron had left off. It was obvious to her now, that's where she'd gotten stuck.

Hale helped Jenna into the passenger seat of the car, making sure she was comfortable before closing the door and coming around to the driver's side. Diane at last felt her ire, her long-held indignation, seep out of her. It was pointless. Plus, she felt ashamed. She had not risen to the occasion as she'd always planned if their paths had ever crossed, but had reverted to the spoiled girl Hale had once accused her of being. She had not been able to bridge the gap of years since their last meeting but he had. He had moved on and put her behind him.

His car moved out ahead of her and Diane followed

as she'd been instructed. It galled her that she was now
beholden to Hale.

They were surprisingly close to the highway entrance,
and he stuck his hand out the window indicating the
right ramp. Hale then changed lanes, giving her space
to pull around his car. She saw that Hale continued to
wait, making sure she was well on her way.

At the last minute Diane flashed her headlights as a
thank-you before picking up speed. This was something
else he could hold over her, no matter how trivial.

Chapter 2

Diane stood at the nursing counter, dressed in a pair of slim black slacks and a dove-gray cashmere turtleneck sweater with fashionable black leather boots. Simple pearl ear studs were her only jewelry. Not exactly holiday colors, she realized when she dressed that morning. Christmas was in the air but she was not about to act like a walking advertisement.

There were makeshift vases of holly and evergreens, wreaths made of fake fruit and poinsettia plants on the counters and a sprig of mistletoe over the entrance to the visitor's lounge. Cutout foil snowflakes were taped to doors and mirrors. It was hard to avoid. But Diane also knew she just wasn't feeling it yet.

"Hey. Haven't seen you lately. When did you cut your hair?" the nursing supervisor asked, sitting at her terminal and working on her computer keyboard.

"About a month ago," Diane answered absently,

focused on the paperwork in front of her. "I got tired of dealing with it. Too much work."

"You look different." The nursing supervisor nodded.

Diane shook her head, amused. "Thanks. I think."

Her hair was trimmed short across her nape but was layered full at the crown and sides, framing a light brown face that was youthful and animated. And except for the unbuttoned traditional white lab coat and the stethoscope folded into one of the pockets there was nothing else about her appearance or posture to indicate she was a doctor.

At that moment she was multitasking, checking messages on her BlackBerry, listening to voice mail from an earpiece and quickly checking off on a hospital form the procedures she'd followed with her last patient. She was also sucking on a piece of candy cane, rolling it around her mouth.

"What are you doing here, anyway? You're not even on the schedule." She checked to make sure.

Diane consulted her BlackBerry once more. She entered a text message before finally turning it off and dropping it into her pocket along with the earpiece.

"I was called in for two late referrals that couldn't wait, according to the attending physicians. The referrals turned into one emergency and the other required a full workup. And there was a bunch of as-long-as-you're-here-doctor-can-you-take-a-look-at-this requests. You know how it is." She sighed.

She wasn't about to admit there was more on her mind than just the obvious routine of her work. To be honest, over the past week or so she found her work was actually a blessed distraction. The horrible events of two years ago notwithstanding, what was on her mind right now was merely irritating. It had kept her awake on three different nights in the last two weeks. It was because she'd seen Hale Cameron again.

Why did he have to be there? she'd been asking herself ever since.

With Jenna.

Who was pregnant.

The image of the friendly woman with her rounded belly evoked a primal reaction in Diane that she, even now, couldn't understand. Pensive, she played with her hair and massaged her scalp with her fingertips.

"Well, if you're finished with patients it's time to get the spirit. Ho ho ho and all that. There's food in the staff lounge. Unless you have a date and you're eating later. Or is that long face because he canceled?"

Diane silently shook her head. The mention of any kind of celebrating for the holidays only made her think of Trevor. Her ex-husband. The gnawing memory made her feel more annoyed than sad.

She leaned her whole torso over the counter as she searched along the desk. "Got anymore candy?"

The nurse playfully swatted her hand. "Leave that alone. It's bad for you."

Diane chuckled quietly but obeyed.

"You didn't answer my question. A dinner date?"

The basket was now beyond her reach and Diane stood up and leaned a hip against the counter. "That's over," she said smoothly, watching the traffic around the nursing station, the passing of staff, patients and visitors trolling the hallways. Many were wearing cheap, felt Santa hats with fuzzy white trim.

The nurse squinted at her in disbelief. "Over? I thought you just met him a few months ago. What happened? If you don't mind me asking."

Diane studied her nails. Her fingers were long and well shaped. Her nails short by necessity, manicured but free of polish. Free of rings, wedding, engagement or friendship.

"It wasn't a good fit. We weren't on the same page about a lot of things."

"He was cute. You threw him outta bed?" The nurse was again incredulous.

Diane's answering smile was faint. "That wasn't it. He was just so…so…*straight*." She struggled to find the right word. "He was nice and all that, but…"

She stopped and frowned, realizing she was about to make an honest confession that she would later have regretted. It didn't help that in the middle of the nurse's probing and her defensive dodging Hale Cameron again came to mind, disrupting her thoughts.

She was seeing Hale as he'd momentarily stood alone and unaware of being observed by her, or anyone, at the end of the gala in Baltimore. She was reminded of when he was nineteen, not long after he'd appeared in her life and become her nemesis.

He had a provocative, strongly defined physique on the cusp of becoming a man. He stood and moved his body in an arrogant posturing way back then, as if he were fully aware of his own assets but wanted to give the impression that he wasn't. But sometimes, Diane recalled, when he didn't know anyone was watching, Hale could seem almost shy, even awkward. That night a few weeks ago, she'd caught a glimpse of that same momentary uncertainty, all pretenses under wraps.

"I guess I'm too busy to concentrate on a relationship right now," Diane said restlessly, forcing the memory to recede.

"That mean you're coming alone to the holiday party?"

"I…have other plans," she improvised.

"Then you should at least stop upstairs before you leave."

"What's upstairs?" Diane asked, again pulling out her BlackBerry to check for messages. She stood reading one, frowning over its contents.

"The kids' party up on six. Santa's coming in to meet them and give out presents."

Diane turned off the phone. "I'm glad you reminded me. I have some things in my car."

Pushing away from the counter, Diane walked toward the elevator. She spoke briefly to colleagues she met in passing, listening to excited plans for Christmas and New Year's, and being asked about her own. She made them up as required.

Without stopping to get her coat, Diane left the building and walked to her car in the staff lot. It was a cold, overcast day, promising rain or snow. She opened the trunk of her car and removed a shopping bag from which protruded two gifts wrapped in kid-friendly holiday paper. She started back toward the building and then suddenly stopped midstride. Returning to her car, Diane opened the driver's side and climbed in, shutting the door behind her. She absently placed the bag on the other seat, pulled out her phone and made a call. She sat with her eyes closed waiting for the connection, thinking about what she was going to say.

"Hi, Eva. It's me."

"Diane. Honey, is everything okay?"

"Yes. I'm sorry I didn't get back to you right away…"

"I know you're very busy at the hospital but I worry when nearly a week goes by…."

Diane let her head drop back against the headrest and slouched in the seat.

"I know." She sighed

"It's just work, right?"

Diane gnawed on her lip, staring out beyond the windshield to the stark evidence of December and that-time-of-the-year.

"Yeah. Mostly," she finally confessed.

There was a silence on the other end and Diane knew what was coming next. She'd hoped to avoid this conversation. Her father would have left it alone, never one to mix it up in her business. But her stepmother, in many ways, knew her better than Adam.

"I know what you're going through right now. That's why I want to know if you'll be coming for Christmas. Bailey is driving me crazy asking every ten minutes when you'll arrive."

Diane smiled at the mention and image of her half sister.

"What should I tell her? And your father?"

She sighed. "Eva…I…don't think I'll make it down. I've waited so long to get a flight it's going to cost me a fortune. Plus I have a couple of cases I have to keep close tabs on. Maybe I can see everyone for a weekend after the holidays are over. I mean, you live only a couple of hours from me."

"That certainly hasn't meant we see you any more frequently. Here's the thing. We want to see you for the holidays, not after. We want you with us. Unless…are you going to stay with your mother this year?"

Diane shook her head even though Eva couldn't see the action. "No, I'm not doing that."

"I understand," Eva murmured.

Diane knew that she did. Eva was kindness itself and would never dream of saying anything critical about Diane's natural mother, even though it was common knowledge that Maron Fairchild was a bit of a drama queen.

"Listen. I know this is a difficult time for you, honey. One of the biggest family holidays of the year and you probably only remember Trevor telling you he's leaving, two days before Christmas."

Diane's stomach roiled with exactly that memory....

At the end of a party they'd given. Their apartment had been jumping with wall-to-wall people, music and laughter. Most of their friends, an equal number of colleagues, his and hers, and even a few total strangers who'd somehow crashed. It was almost 2:00 a.m. when she'd closed the door on the last guest. Eva was wrong about one part of the story. Trevor had never told her he was leaving. After making a feeble attempt to clean up some of the debris and leftovers of their party she'd realized that it was suddenly very quiet and Trevor was nowhere to be seen.

"Trevor? Where are you? How about giving me a hand?"

She'd found him in their bedroom. Packing a suitcase.

Diane no longer remembered if he said anything just then or even what she'd said to him. But she would never forget his simple response to her annoyed accusation that he was being childish as he silently picked up the case, calmly walked to a hall closet and put on his coat. Finally, opening the apartment door.

"Goodbye, Diane."

That was it.

You'll hear from my lawyer had been posted in an e-mail to her several days later.

The echo of Trevor's words still felt like a raw open wound. And just this week, a few days before Christmas, it felt worse believing she was destined to relive that awful moment, forever.

"I know you think that's the reason, and I appreciate your concern, Eva. But the truth is, I do have some patients with serious issues."

"I believe you but I don't believe that means you can't get away to spend Christmas with your family. Come down for just a few days. Leave the day after Christmas if you really have to."

Diane silently chuckled. "You're making me feel so guilty."

"I hope so. You don't need to be alone. You don't need to punish yourself that way. Bailey is making all kinds of plans. Hayden keeps hinting at something in particular he's sure you're getting him. Adam wants to know if he needs to rent a second Jeep. We invited Simon and I think he's coming, too."

"Simon," she repeated, surprised. "You'll never see him. He's going to be breaking hearts all over the island."

"I know, but I trust your father to keep him in line, if that's called for. And, honey, *I* really want to see you. Come home."

Come home.

"I don't want to make any promises…" Diane stopped and swallowed, stunned by the sudden lump in her throat and the uncharacteristic urge to cry. She cleared her throat. "Look…I took a moment to call you back so you wouldn't think I was avoiding you…"

"But you were…"

"There's a holiday party going on right now in the pediatric ward and I'm late."

"Then go. Just don't forget we're all here for you."

"Say hi to everybody for me."

"Take care, sweetie. Love you."

"Love you, too."

Diane ended the call but just sat there. She couldn't move just then if her life depended on it. She was a pile of tender nerves, confused emotions, convoluted but vivid memories. She felt perilously close to tears and hated that she could lose control while sitting pathetically in her car, in a hospital parking lot, just days before Christmas. Alone.

She muttered an oath and scrambled out of the car, snatching up the bag with the gifts. With her head high and any suspicion of tears swept away by the wind, Diane went to join the festivities in the children's ward.

"Hey. You made it."

"Hi, Ron. Sorry I'm so late but the children's party at the hospital threw me off schedule. You probably thought I was going to stand you up."

The burly black man, his dark face wreathed in a grin from cheek to cheek, let out a rumble of laughter.

"You could never be too late. I appreciate you could squeeze in some time for us. Come on in and sit a minute. But be careful." Ron pointed meaningfully to a small bouquet of greenery taped just above his door.

"What is it?" Diane asked.

"Mistletoe. Only but two or three of us know what it is and what it's for. Hasn't been used yet."

"Your idea, I suppose."

"Hey, it's a good way to teach about another Christmas tradition, right? It's not all about the gifts and turkey."

Diane shook her head wryly and did as she was told, maneuvering around the stacks of boxes, flyers, folders and other sundry this and that that pretty much filled Ron Jeffrey's office. She sat on an inverted milk carton since the second chair in the office had transit files piled on it. She unwound the long scarf fashionably twisted around her neck and shrugged out of her coat. Ron squeezed his bulk around a corner of the desk and plopped into his chair. He pushed his glasses up his nose while quickly and efficiently checking e-mails on his surely about-to-die aging PC and answering his telephone. He dispensed with two calls and the messages and then pushed back in his chair to regard Diane with a warm smile.

"Thanks for coming, Diane. Hope I didn't pull you away from anything important."

"You didn't. I didn't need to spend too much time at that party. I nearly overdosed on Christmas candy and hot chocolate."

Ron laughed again, the sound carrying out his office door and down the halls of the shelter where a valiant attempt had been made to make the place look festive and cheerful.

"Can't offer you hot chocolate. Milk is too expensive. But the market two blocks away donated a couple of cartons of apple juice for our party. Care to have some? I can put a little fortifier in it, if you want, against the cold," he said, winking at her.

"Not yet." She laughed. "I'd like to first take a look at the boy and senior resident you're concerned about."

"Good idea. Then you have to meet Santa Claus. If

you've been a good little girl, maybe he's got somethin' for you in his sack."

That sent him off into another peel of uproarious laughter. Diane enjoyed his spirit. He was director of the community shelter for displaced families. She'd always been impressed not only by Ron's advocacy on behalf of the homeless, but his amazing ability to get services and favors from the most unlikely places when most other people could not. She suspected that people were afraid of Ron Jeffrey because of his size and very commanding voice. She wouldn't put it past him to exaggerate both if it got results for the shelter. Over time she'd come to know him as the gentlest of men, and a very savvy and smart one. He seemed to deliberately let his appearance belie the fact that he held a master's degree in not-for-profit administration.

Diane glanced around the office. "Is this the only private space?"

He shook his head, pursing his lips. "No such thing as privacy in a place like this, I'm afraid."

"Then this is fine."

She opened the leather satchel she'd brought with her and began to remove equipment and instruments. Without a word Ron sprang up from his desk and left the office, closing the usually open door behind him.

In just a few minutes he returned, escorting an older white woman into the office, offering Diane a quick introduction to Nan. He left, with a silent jerk of his head to indicate he'd be within shouting distance if she needed his help.

The woman was mostly silent, asking no questions, offering no earlier information, sitting passively while Diane did a basic exam of her vital signs. She didn't even seem particularly interested in what Diane was doing.

Ron had informed her that the older woman recently seemed incoherent.

Diane made quiet idle talk for reassurance to the woman who, she could well imagine, probably hadn't seen a doctor in years. Two very simple little movements requested of the woman quickly confirmed her suspicions.

"Okay, Nan, I think I'm done," Diane said.

"Can I…now?" the woman asked.

"Give me a few more minutes."

The woman nodded, staring blankly into space.

Diane managed to reach the door from her position behind it, and opened it to signal Ron, who stood talking with a resident near the reception desk.

"How's it going?" Ron asked.

"I want to get her to the emergency room tonight for a more thorough exam."

"What's up?"

"I suspect a ministroke. There was at least one but there might have been more. I don't think we should wait until the morning."

"No problem. I'll have someone drive her over right now."

"Good." Diane nodded briskly.

She used Ron's desk phone to call the hospital to alert them to Nan's arrival and to give her authorization that she be seen immediately.

"Come on, Nan. We're going to take you for a little ride. Would you like that?" Ron asked.

Her eyes briefly lit up and she nodded.

"Before you go," Diane said, retrieving something else from her bag. It was a small, flat, wrapped gift she held out to the woman. "Merry Christmas."

"Ooooh. Like. Thank…you."

She hugged the gift to her chest, smiling for the first time.

Ron turned her by the shoulders to guide her from the office.

"That was really cool of you to have something for Nan. She has no family, far as we know."

"It's just a little thing. I had an extra gift after taking care of some of my staff. Where's the boy?"

"Look, you're going to have to go to him."

Diane frowned. "Why?"

"There's a party goin' on, and he's not about to leave right now. We got Santa and everything."

Diane laughed in understanding. "Okay. Lead the way."

She took only her stethoscope with her as she followed Ron. There was music and a lot of loud conversation coming from a space at the end of a corridor. The noise from the other end only got louder as they approached. There was a room to the left that turned out to be the communal dining hall.

At the back of the room, near the door, the adults stood or sat watching the excitement of perhaps fifty children and adolescents at the front of the room as they waited to meet with Santa Claus and receive a gift.

Diane couldn't help but smile at the cheerful chaos as kids roughhoused together, or shouted to be next, or played with gifts already opened, or sat staring dumbfounded at the man at the center of attention, Santa Claus.

She began to chuckle when she realized he was the tallest, thinnest Santa she'd ever seen. Not that that mattered to the kids. He was seated in a chair raised on an improvised platform. For all their hardships and deprivations, the children clearly believed in this Santa who'd made a special trip from the North Pole just to see them.

"That's Qa'Shawn over there. The kid jumping up and down. I told him not to do that," Ron said, worried.

"That's actually a good sign."

"Well, let me go get him. I told him someone special wanted to meet him 'cause he passed out yesterday. He thinks he did something special," he said, bemused.

Diane found a little spot by herself out of the way of the celebration. It was a moment before she became aware that Santa appeared to be sending covert glances at her. But then he went back to being jolly and attentive to the kids. They seemed to find it pretty cool that he was a black Santa behind the snow-white beard. He cast her another long look and then ignored her.

"Qa'Shawn, this is Dr. Diane. I told you about her. Say hello." Ron gave the youngster a light nudge.

"Hello," the boy murmured.

He was maybe nine years old.

"Hi, Qa'Shawn." Diane smiled at him.

"You a doctor for real?"

"I am." She held out her stethoscope. "See."

"I know what that is. You listen to a heart with that. Can I try it?"

Diane placed the ear tips of the headset lightly into his ears and then put the diaphragm against the boy's chest. After just a few seconds his eyes grew wide.

"I hear noise in there. Is that my heart?"

"Hope so," Ron said. "If you don't hear anything you're in deep trouble."

But the boy was too fascinated with the sounds coming through the instrument to try and figure out Ron's macabre joke.

"Can I listen, too?" Diane asked.

Qa'Shawn relinquished the headset to her. Diane put it to her own ears and listened, using the tunable diaphragm to make adjustments. After a minute Diane removed the headset, looping the stethoscope around her neck. She grinned at Qa'Shawn. "Sounds like a lot of rushing water to me."

The boy laughed but was already getting antsy to get away.

"I don't want to keep you from Santa. Nice meeting you, Qa'Shawn."

He shouted goodbye and took off like a shot.

"Well?" Ron asked in a quiet voice.

"I hear a murmur. Could mean his heartbeat's a little irregular. It's not unusual and it's not normally dangerous, but I'd like to see Qa'Shawn at the hospital."

Ron frowned. "Not tonight."

"No, it can wait until after the holidays, but I'd like to run some tests to see what we're dealing with."

Ron nodded solemnly. "I'll make sure it happens. Anyway, if we try to pull him away before Hale finishes his Santa act…"

"Hale?" she asked faintly.

"Yeah. Hale Cameron. Good buddy of mine. I had to beg big-time to get him here, and threaten him if he didn't wear the suit. I can't help that it's too big."

Diane had already turned her attention back to the front of the room where Hale, unrecognizable under the Santa garb, was acting the part and talking the talk and keeping a lot of children very entertained. Except for those few moments when he was distracted by her presence, Hale was all about the business of being Santa Claus.

"He owed me a favor and I called it in," Ron continued. "But he would have done it in the end. I just had to work on him a bit." Ron laughed. "I want you to meet him."

At that Diane headed out of the room, back to Ron's office. "Some other time. He's busy and I should be going."

"Well, I'm not going to keep you. You're probably on your way to a party right now."

Not, Diane thought to herself.

They'd almost reached Ron's office when he was called aside by a resident complaining that someone had stolen his sneakers and backpack. Ron had to deal with it. Diane quickly got her coat and bag. Running into Hale Cameron twice in as many weeks was starting to make her feel cursed. Before she got to the door, her BlackBerry silently signaled there were messages once she was back to the hospital.

Her position didn't allow her to ignore them. Perching on the edge of Ron's desk, Diane scrolled through her e-mails and text messages. Fortunately, there was no emergency, just several colleagues wishing her a happy holiday and friends inviting her to join them for drinks. There was another invitation to yet another party, and a request for the name of a particular doctor.

Totally wrapped up in responding, she paid no attention to the voices and conversation in the hallway. Diane was just finishing her last post when one voice stood out distinctly from the rest. She was instantly spurred into action, and she scrambled to grab her things and get away. The door was ajar and she put her hand out to pull it open. It was pushed from the other side, forcing her to step back quickly.

Santa Claus filled the doorway.

Silently, her heart palpitating with a fight-or-flight reflex, Diane stared at the man behind the guise. For a very long moment neither said anything and it was impossible for her to tell what was going through Hale's mind since she couldn't see all of his face or much of his eyes. She also made the quick observation of how funny he looked behind the fake snow-white beard.

Standing so close in front of him, she could smell the storage chemicals on the rented Santa suit and she could smell Hale's cologne or aftershave. Plus a little bit of male heat.

"'Scuse me," she murmured, not looking into his face as she tried to slide past him through the doorway.

"No problem," he murmured back.

"Don't move! Perfect! Man, I couldn't plan this."

Curious, Diane looked at Ron. He pointed to the door frame over her and Hale's head. He looked up, too. The evergreen bouquet was fixed and ready. Ron burst out into loud, satisfied laughter.

"Don't just stand there," he encouraged. "You're supposed to kiss each other."

Diane's gaze flew to Hale's, her eyes wide with surprise. And fear. She was about to protest but never got the chance.

Hale suddenly seemed to swoop forward and she couldn't move. The thick wooly beard was ridiculous, but soft and kind of ticklish. Through it she felt the firm, warm pressure of his mouth.

Chapter 3

Hale's lips did not meet hers.

He kissed, instead, a corner of her mouth. Tantalizingly close, but safe and chaste.

And it was quick.

For Diane, it was that...and, oddly, seemed to take a very long time.

When Hale withdrew, standing back against the open door, Ron began to clap his big hands in loud and sustained approval. The sound seemed to echo somewhere in the back of her brain. Her heart was beating too fast, and even Diane recognized it was because of unexpected heightened emotions. Why was she just standing there, staring at...Santa?

Finally, the sounds of her surroundings, the noise and conversations and closing of doors and crying of babies rushed full force at her, until it all seemed too loud.

"...so I can make a formal intro between you two."

"What?" Diane asked absently.

"I said—" Ron began, only to be interrupted.

"I've got to get out of this suit," Hale announced firmly. He allowed Diane to pass and closed the office door on both of them.

Diane scowled at Ron. He was beaming at her.

"So now you've met Hale. That was quite an introduction."

"Yes, it was," Diane said with as much grace as she could muster. "But I have to go."

"I know, I know," Ron conceded with regret.

He spread his arms that seemed to have the wingspan of a bald eagle. Diane, smiling in amusement, accepted his warm hug and thanks.

"I'd be happy to come by when I'm free and do a brief checkup on anyone you think needs it, Ron."

He placed an affectionate hand on her shoulder as Diane headed to the exit.

"Hell, they all need it, Diane. You know these folks don't have any health care. Anything you can do is always appreciated." He patted her shoulder and waved her off.

Outside, Diane inhaled deeply several times, grateful for the sudden rush of cold air on her face. She headed toward her car, feeling bewildered by the experience of seeing him at the shelter playing the part of one of humankind's most beloved icons. Right up there with Mickey Mouse. And Jesus.

The contradiction only confused her more.

Diane put her things in the trunk of her car and sat for a while as the engine warmed her. She stared blindly out the window. It was almost nine in the evening, four days before Christmas. There weren't that many people about, but then it was cold and she was not in a highly commercial part of town. It was a depressed area that could sorely use gentrification…if anyone, resident or government official, could agree on the need for it.

The shelter was little more than a storefront, with the upper floors roughly converted into dorm-like rooms and shared facilities. It felt enormously sad to Diane that families, *children*, had to call this place home, let alone spend the holidays here.

People like Ron Jeffrey should be canonized, she considered. But with that also came the image of Hale in the Santa suit. Was he to be blessed, as well?

She was pondering this when the object of her thoughts exited the shelter, dressed down in dark casual slacks, heavy hiking boots, a barn jacket and baseball cap. A dark green-and-red plaid scarf was his only concession to the holidays. Leather gloves stuck out of a pocket of his coat.

She had never seen Hale like this, with the young black professional look, decidedly upwardly mobile. Nice clothes of good quality and well coordinated. Stylish. And handsome.

No, that wasn't true. Diane remembered her surprise at seeing how well Hale filled out a formal tux at the affair in Baltimore. She frowned as her gaze followed his brisk pace. His car keys ready, he pointed and clicked and the lights of a black SUV blinked on.

Hale was climbing into his car when Diane, spontaneous, bold, determined and without a clue of what she was actually going to do, turned off her engine, got out of her car and hurried across the parking lot toward his.

"Hale! Hale, wait a minute."

He stopped in midaction, turning his head to watch as she approached. Diane slowed her steps. She suddenly realized that Hale's expression, what she could see of it in the shadows and under the eerie florescent public lights, showed him tight-lipped. His eyes were hooded. He didn't say a word but watched her warily.

"I want to say something," Diane announced.

He put his hand up to stop her. She did.

"Look, I'm sorry. Ron put us on the spot. I shouldn't have touched you. So, if you want..."

Diane shook her head. "No, that's not what this is about. Ron meant well. It's the holidays and all that. You know."

"Yes. I know."

He still sounded suspicious.

"I..." She made a vague gesture with her hand. "I just want to say...you were so great with the kids."

Hale stared silently at her.

"I mean, it was great. And...and dressing up like Santa. You're kind of thin for the part...."

"Is that a compliment?" he asked dryly.

She chuckled nervously, rubbing her hands together, trying to figure out how to end the conversation that she'd begun.

"I guess it didn't sound like one," Diane agreed.

Hale wasn't doing or saying anything to make this easy for her. He wasn't being conciliatory or even friendly. Diane sighed. She couldn't blame him. Two weeks ago when the tables were turned she'd given him no quarter either. In fact, she knew her response to seeing him after so many years had been way over the top.

"If you're finished, I have to go," he said, once again turning to his car.

"How's Jenna?"

He turned sharply and pinned her with a cold stare. "Why do you want to know?"

Diane was shocked by his tone, as if she'd asked something highly personal. She shrugged, becoming annoyed that he continued to treat her like a pariah.

"When I met her she was very pregnant. I only wanted to know if everything is okay. I have a professional interest," she quickly tacked on.

"Jenna is fine. The baby was born about a week ago. Twenty-four hours before her due date."

Diane felt a little strange just then. Something had been irrevocably set in time. Hale's future seemed fixed and tied to two other people in his life.

"That's…" She stopped and forced a smile. "That's great. Boy or girl?"

"A boy," Hale responded, relaxing only a bit. "They're both good. It was an easy delivery."

"She's lucky."

"Right." He nodded, was momentarily distracted. Abruptly he again started to get into his car.

"Any name yet?"

Patiently, Hale stood and turned to her. "Quinn. Elliott is the middle name. It's a family name."

"Quinn. I like that."

"Are you done?" he asked softly.

"I was only trying—"

"Yeah, I got that," he interrupted, arching a brow.

"Yes, I'm done. I wish you, Jenna and the baby all the best. Your wife is very lovely. What a great—"

"What did you say?" He frowned deeply.

Diane stared at him. "I was talking about your wife. Okay, I'm sorry. Girlfriend. Significant other. Baby Mama. Whatever." She was feeling defensive again.

His mouth and jaw clinched tightly. His eyes were

dark with a dangerous glint barely visible under the visor of his cap. She suddenly couldn't take her gaze from Hale's face. It was transforming, going through several different emotions but settling on something akin to resignation. Or defeat. Or even disappointment.

What did he have to be disappointed about?

She didn't want to know.

"Sorry I bothered you. Good night, Hale. Congratulations," Diane muttered, through with pleasantries. She turned to head back to her own car.

"Do you have to be someplace right now?"

She slowed and glanced back at him, puzzled. "Excuse me? No. I don't have any plans. Why?"

"I need you to come with me. It won't take long. Thirty minutes, tops. Get in."

Diane's mouth dropped open at this blunt delivery. Clearly Hale didn't expect her to say no. He was already in the driver's seat and had turned on the ignition. The motor idled. He waited.

Curiosity getting the better of her, Diane walked around to the passenger side and climbed in. She'd barely closed her door before Hale was on the accelerator, driving out of the lot.

"Where are you taking me?"

"If you were really concerned you wouldn't have gotten in. Put on your seat belt and enjoy the ride."

He said not another word. And although she was completely mystified as to where Hale was going, she felt no fear. Several times Diane cast long searching looks at his profile. The clenching of his jaw had not let up. He was upset about something but she couldn't even guess at what.

Ten minutes later Hale's car turned down a residential street of row houses. They were beautiful in architectural design but many were in need of repair and restoration. A few were being worked on. One was boarded up. The car slowed in front of a limestone, the entrance door light a welcome beacon on the otherwise dark street. He parallel parked and got out. Then he stood on the sidewalk silently waiting for her to join him.

"Is this where you live?" she asked.

Hale continued to ignore her question. He started up the stairs to the entrance and rang the bell twice. He waited about fifteen seconds before using a set of keys to unlock the door and slowly open it.

"Jenna?" he called in. "Are you home?" He stood waiting just inside a small mudroom space.

Diane, standing just behind Hale, was suddenly sorry she'd agreed to accompany him. From somewhere inside, a small voice called out. Diane could hear no more than, "I'm in the back.'"

"It's me," Hale shouted back.

He stepped inside and Diane followed. The first thing she saw was a brand-new baby stroller. Hale stood in the center of the foyer, a staircase to his right and an open room to the left, like a parlor or front salon room. Diane noticed there wasn't a lot of furniture. No hung pictures although some were framed and leaning against the walls. There was a rolled-up area rug and packed boxes. It was hard to tell if someone was moving in or moving out.

A small figure appeared at the end of the hallway from the back of the house.

"I'm glad you're here. Who's that with you?"

"I brought someone who wants to see the baby."

Hale gave Diane only a cursory glance and he didn't see the surprised widening of her eyes. That hadn't been her wish at all.

"You've met her before," Hale said, beckoning to the petite woman, who now joined them near the front door.

Jenna appeared, small and lithe, dressed in jeans and a black sweater. Her hair looked like it hadn't been combed, but was gathered haphazardly, twisted and secured with a clip. She was completely fresh faced and without makeup and looked incredibly young, sweet and pretty. She had on slippers…and was holding a very small bundle up to one shoulder, her new baby, gently petting him on the back. Jenna greeted them with a pleased smile but immediately reached up to Hale, who had to bend quite a way to accommodate her as they hugged.

Diane averted her gaze, pretending an interest in the pattern on the wood parquet floors.

"We met in Baltimore," Jenna said to Diane.

"Yes. Yes." Diane nodded foolishly. Hale then suddenly, carefully, took the baby out of Jenna's arms.

"Diane was at the shelter tonight," Hale said as he gazed upon the tiny baby in the crook of his arm.

Jenna laughed. "I bet he looked like something else in that Santa suit. When he told me what he was doing I had to laugh. I wish I could have seen that."

Diane smiled slightly. "He did a good job. You would have been proud of him."

Jenna looked vaguely puzzled.

The baby squirmed and fussed and fell silent again.

"Can I see?"

Diane stepped next to Hale and he obligingly tilted his arms so that she could peel back a thin, pale yellow baby blanket and peer into the sleeping face of the week-old infant.

She saw babies all the time on her rounds, with private patients and at clinics and shelters. They came in all shapes, colors and sizes, with and without hair. But they were still largely anonymous. Unless there was a problem that required additional visits or further treatments, the small wizened faces became somewhat interchangeable to Diane. But she found herself staring at this child, studying him and the sweet peacefulness of his face. A tiny fist was curled closed and sticking out of the folds of the blanket. She was tempted to reach out and...

"You don't mind, do you?"

Diane realized that Jenna and Hale were looking at her. One had asked her a question.

"I'm sorry. What did you say?"

"I need Hale's help. Will you watch the baby? Just for a few minutes."

"I...well...sure."

Hale stood poised to pass the sleeping child to her. Diane hastily took off her coat and turned to accept the baby. As Hale also removed his coat and baseball cap, she moved to a nearby chair and sat down. Hale and Jenna left her alone.

The baby slept. He was breathing softly, now and then working his little mouth in a small sucking motion. The fist open, the fingers stretched and then closed again. He sighed and kicked a leg as he slept. He was so small and warm.

Diane was fascinated. She could not remember the last time she'd actually sat like this and held a baby. Maybe when Bailey or Hayden were babies. She let her gaze roam his perfect features, looking for the parts that were like Jenna. And the parts that were like Hale.

She had no idea how much time lapsed before

they returned to the front room, deep in a serious conversation. Hale was instructing Jenna who to call about a malfunctioning refrigerator.

"I'm not going to fool with it, Jen. It's probably the thermostat. Sorry it wasn't an easy fix."

"Me, too." Jenna sighed. "Especially with having to keep prepared bottles of his milk and formula."

She reached to take her son from Diane, who released him but then sat feeling somewhat useless. She quickly stood to put her coat back on.

"I thought men knew how to fix anything that ran on power."

"My husband is actually very good at that. Unfortunately, he's on the other side of the world," Jenna chuckled as she soothed the infant who was whimpering. She bounced him gently in her arms.

Diane stared at her. Then she looked at Hale. His expression said it all. She'd made a big mistake and a colossal fool of herself.

"Really? Where is he?"

"Iraq. Second tour of duty, but he got promoted to captain. You can see what happened when he was home the last time," Jenna said wryly as she smiled, besotted, at her son. "He left me with a special package. Thank goodness for Skype, video calls and Hale. Colby got to see his son just hours after he was born. He said it was the best Christmas present ever."

Diane didn't dare look at Hale again. He didn't have to say anything. Jenna had innocently, effectively, absolved him of all the transgressions she'd blindly heaped upon him.

"I'd say so," Diane murmured.

"When are your parents arriving?" Hale asked Jenna.

"Tomorrow evening. They'll be here for two weeks so I'll get a lot done around here with their help. As you can see, Diane, I'm just moving in. I don't have family in D.C. but this is Colby's home. I'm so glad I had Hale to help me before Quinn came along.

"My mother is going to enjoy hanging pictures, but mostly I know she and Dad want to spend time with their first grandchild," she continued.

"What about your in-laws?" Diane asked.

"Colby's mom will join us next weekend. Only one missing is Colby."

Diane knew she wasn't mistaken when she heard the little catch and crack in Jenna's voice.

"I hope he returns soon," she said softly. "He's got so much waiting for him. He's lucky."

"Me, too." Jenna nodded. She turned to reach out a hand to Hale who took it. "Hale is one of Colby's best friends, and he's been wonderful to me. But I'm sure you know what a good man he is."

Diane swallowed. She knew if she tried to say anything she would go up in flames on the spot for not being honest. She glanced at Hale.

He didn't look any less angry with her.

"I gotta run," he said, kissing the back of Jenna's hand. "I have to take Diane back to her car."

"I'm glad you brought her along."

"Congratulations to you and your husband."

Diane stepped outside into the cold December night. She filled her lungs with the crisp air, trying to clear her head. But it was going to take far more than that to snap her out of it. Behind her, Hale and Jenna said their goodbyes, and then Hale was closing the door as he joined her. Without a word he headed back to the parked SUV. Diane followed as if her feet were encased in lead.

Nothing flip or smart came to mind that she could say to dispel the tension between them. What she had already said could not be unsaid. And she knew Hale was not going to forget.

Hale drove into the parking lot outside the shelter and pulled up next to her car. He turned off his engine and a silence fell upon them. They both sat staring out the windshield. Beyond, there was the start of a light fall of snow.

"I'm sorry. It was wrong to assume…what I did," Diane said simply. But she doubted Hale believed her. She couldn't blame him.

He sighed, shaking his head.

"What is it with you? You still hold my past against me, don't you? My family and where I came from. Your father taking an interest in me. You've always resented me, Diane. Thought the worst of me. Believed I'm just not good enough."

"Hale, that's—"

"Don't even try to say that's not true," he said sharply, turning to stare at her profile. "At least be honest about how you really feel. Let's put it out there, in the open, and deal with it. Then maybe we can both move on. You hate me."

She felt cold, the blood seeming to drain from her face. There was little she could say to refute Hale's accusation. And now that he'd said it out loud, she knew he was right. Mixed with her guilt was also shame. Hale had so managed to trap her with her own behavior.

"It's…not that black-and-white and you know it," she said defensively.

"Oh. You mean you had every right to be suspicious

of me then. Okay, I'll give you that. I could have become a bum, but I grew up. I had a great second chance to change my life and I did. But you just don't see that. Or you don't want to."

"Well, I haven't seen you in years," she responded, annoyed.

"You made sure that you wouldn't."

Diane's gaze riveted to him. "How do you know that?"

"I know you. I know how you feel about me. I didn't want to do anything to create more bad blood between us. So I did just the opposite. I went out of my way to let bygones be bygones. I even wanted to invite you to my graduation. Your father said he didn't think that was a good idea. Was he wrong?"

Stunned, Diane remained silent. At the time, no.

"Did you know your parents threw me a party when I passed the bar exam?"

Law school.

No. She didn't know about that either.

"You were never interested in my life or what I could become. I understand why."

"Why?" she challenged him.

"Because of this…"

And with that, Hale turned partially in his seat, placed a hand behind Diane's head and forced her to meet his kiss.

It was not a rough crushing of his mouth to hers, or a use of brute strength to subdue her. But her surprise at his sudden movement forced her mouth open as she gasped in protest. Hale took full advantage as he locked his lips to hers, invading the warm cavern with his tongue. He staked a claim and took over.

Diane made a feeble attempt to free herself, her hand

pushing against his chest. But then, the stroking and stirring of Hale's tongue, the sheer mastery of his control and affect, seemed to magically dissolve her resistance. That gave way rather quickly to her full cooperation, allowing him full access and engaging his tongue with her own. Diane began to feel as if every nerve ending in her body was electrified.

Unlike the swift start of the kiss, Hale was very slow and deliberate in how he ended it. His moist lips clung to hers a moment longer until she felt only his warm breath against her.

Hale abruptly released her and sat back in his seat, staring ahead once again.

Diane tried to recoup, tried to feel put-upon. She was furious with herself. He'd caught her unaware and she'd totally embarrassed herself by giving in.

"That's what you wanted from me when you were seventeen," Hale said quietly. "Then, when you couldn't handle it, when you didn't even know what to do, you got pissed off at *me*."

She remained quiet, his words evoking a time and place and feeling that periodically resurfaced and haunted her.

"I guess I should be grateful that you didn't tell Adam I tried to rape you. My life would have really been over."

She heard the underlying fear in Hale's statement and went suddenly cold. Diane recognized, maybe more than she did as a teenager, that she *could* have ruined him, destroyed his life.

"I didn't know what was going to happen," she said.

"Sure you did," he said wearily. "I was a guinea pig.

You were testing your powers. Thank God for me, you failed."

Diane caught her breath, as if she'd been slapped. She reached for her bag and scarf. "I hope you feel better, now that you've insulted me and said what you've been wanting to say for years."

"You're not insulted. You're mad because I see right through you."

That did it. He'd given her a reason to strike back.

"You know, Jenna's wrong about you. You're not a good man!"

Hale stared at her, his gaze roaming over her face with studied curiosity. Like she was a stranger. Worse, a bug. His eyes were blank suddenly and indifferent.

"Merry Christmas, Diane."

It was the very last thing she was expecting him to say. She'd already steeled herself against another cutting remark, a mean observation. Diane opened her mouth to retaliate. But, for what?

Instead, she struggled to get out of Hale's car and slammed the door behind her.

She felt the pressure of his mouth as he coaxed hers open. Her eyes were closed. It felt so thrilling that way, what he was doing. And his tongue, wet and aggressive, felt strange at first but now was making her feel tingly and ticklish down there, between her legs. She didn't want him to stop. She slid her hands under his shirt, and the feel of his firm bare skin made the sensation swell and grow. Where was it going? How was this going to end? She was breathing hard, feeling her own heart thumping in her chest. His hand was curved around her butt, pulling her tight. He was hard where they pressed together. There was a swirl of something

*new in her stomach. But it felt...good. Delicious and
dangerous. If he kept pushing against her, grinding their
hips together...*

Diane impatiently threw off the quilt. She felt like she
was suffocating. She was sweaty. Then she was hit with
the cool air of her bedroom, even though the baseboard
radiator was releasing heat. She rolled onto her back and
stared overhead. The shadow of the venetian blind at her
window was outlined. Tiny little blurry spots seemed
to be slowly moving across the ceiling. She closed her
eyes tightly, but the dream was gone.

Diane got out of bed and went to the window. Outside
the earlier flakes had turned into a snowfall. There was
three to four inches of the white stuff on the street. All
the cars were covered. And the world was absolutely
silent and still. She wiped at the moisture at her throat
and down between her breasts. She felt damp between
her thighs, up into the apex of her groin.

It was a little after 3:00 a.m.

She stood staring at the beauty beyond her window
and experienced a peculiar and unsettling loneliness.
There were mounted Christmas trees on a number of
terraces of nearby buildings in Adam Morgan where she
lived, and grinning plastic Santa Clauses lit from the
inside. Colorful decorations and garlands of lights were
set to blink and twinkle off and on all night. There were
star-shaped lamps and fake candlesticks in windows.
Diane rubbed her bare arms and turned from the sight.
Her apartment was very dark. There was no evidence
of Christmas anywhere.

It's so much easier this way, she told herself. Without
the constant reminders she could tough out the holidays.
But Diane had underestimated the power of the isolation
she'd imposed upon herself because...

That was the question. Because of…what?

She wandered into her living room and curled into a corner of the sofa, hugging an accent pillow and staring out of the window and hearing over and over again Hale's accusations. Each one seemed to seep into her bones, seemed to be planted in her brain. All of it now seemed in direct contradiction to his kiss.

She felt a swirl of response in the pit of her stomach, a gentle skipping of her heartbeat. She closed her eyes and relived the instant Hale's tongue invaded her mouth and the reaction that she didn't seem able to avoid.

The reliving of those moments continued as she sat in a near stupor, letting it wash over her until dawn. Until first light and her neighborhood came awake for the start of another day. She waited until a little after seven, a time she deemed decent, and then placed the call.

"Hello," a sleepy voice answered.

Diane cringed. "I woke you up. Eva, I'm sorry."

"Hmmmmmm. What time is it?"

"Too early. Go back to sleep. I'll call later."

"Honey, if you're calling now you must have a good reason. What's going on?"

"I'll finish my appointments and rounds today. I'm sure I can change my schedule for tomorrow. There are other doctors to cover my patients.

"I'm coming for Christmas."

Chapter 4

The hydrofoil cut its engines and coasted into the slip next to the pier. Already passengers were crowding the door of the gangway and were backed all the way up the stairs that led to the open upper deck of the craft. Then there was the luggage. Suitcases and baskets and tote bags and boxes and crates of produce and other foodstuffs, piled and ready to be off-loaded.

It was a routine that Hale had seen and experienced before, during a handful of visits to St. John, one of the three U.S. Virgin Islands. However, this was the first time that he found himself in the position of waiting for someone to arrive, instead of the other way around. He wasn't looking forward to the encounter but he was prepared.

Several of the crew jumped to the dock landing, pulling on the heavy ropes to bring the vessel alongside and tie off the lines. The door was promptly opened and people began to file off onto the dock. They searched the bags being unloaded, grabbed their own, and walked off to be greeted by friends or family and driven away to near and far points on the small island. Many were carrying coats or still wearing boots. Many more were dressed in keeping with the tropics. Flip-flops, shorts, tank tops, sunglasses and hats, defenses against the intense heat of the sun. Most were visitors from the mainland, down for the holidays. But other than the comical attempt to string lights across Cruz Bay Square, there was no indication that it was Christmas day.

Hale, leaning back against the grill of the Jeep, slowly made his way to the land end of the pier and dock, standing in the shade as he carefully scanned the disembarking travelers. He was wary, intent on his first sight of Diane, especially given the last time they'd seen each other.

That had been a mistake.

Hale kept telling himself that but he wasn't sure he believed it. It wasn't as if he'd planned to suddenly kiss Diane like that. But it sure had surprised the hell of out him that she'd let him. And responded. Unbelievable. Then there didn't seem to be a reason, a rush, to stop it right away. He just went with it, let his mouth ride hers, drawing from the unexpected encouragement. But when their kiss ended, Hale still knew it hadn't made a bit of difference between them.

Yet he'd been thinking about it ever since.

He restlessly adjusted his black canvas baseball cap, his sunglasses. He stuffed his hands into the pockets of his olive drab cargo shorts, hoping he gave the impression that he didn't care what Diane's reaction was going to be to seeing him. It was her problem, not his.

He began to slowly pace. He frowned, wondering if maybe he'd missed her somehow and she'd gotten past him, was already grabbing a taxi to her parent's house. Then he saw her.

That was when he realized he was wrong. Diane was his problem, too.

He stood watching as she stepped off the ramp from the hydrofoil. She adjusted her oversized and overstuffed tote onto her shoulder. Her suitcase was a not-to-be-missed bright red wheelie. She also had another tote, lumpy and misshapen with its contents, the opening revealing holiday wrappings. And she was carrying a wide-brim straw hat.

Catching her off guard, and unaware that she was being watched, afforded Hale a chance to see Diane with all her defenses down. She looked summery, half of her face lost behind outsized shades. She was wearing jeans with low-heeled boots. Not the skinny kind of designer jeans that did no woman justice, but a pair that flattered Diane's long legs and shapely rear end. She also wore a white short-sleeved shirt, fitted to her torso, the front unbuttoned to the top of her breasts. Underneath was just a peek of a royal-blue cami. The outfit actually made her look cool in the tropical heat of the Caribbean.

He'd noticed in Baltimore that she'd cut her hair. It was a more becoming and sophisticated style for her somewhat square face. At the moment it was tumbled and windblown, but made Diane seem carefree, relaxed and sexy, Hale thought, raising his brows at the idea. That was also blended with the imagery of her when they'd kissed.

Seeing that she was determined but unable to manage all of her belongings, Hale began walking toward her.

"I'll take that," he announced simply, grabbing the

handle of the wheelie and picking up the tote, which was a lot heavier than it looked.

Diane opened her mouth to protest and finally recognized him. He couldn't see her eyes, but her mouth gaped into an *O*.

"How did…what are you doing here?" she asked, her tone reflecting genuine surprise.

"Welcome to St. John," he said. He indicated her bags. "Is this everything?"

Still staring at him, she silently nodded.

"The car's over there," Hale said, and began heading off the pier.

He waited for the indignation and questions to come hurling at his back. There were none. He expected Diane to tell him to put her things down, that she would rather take a cab. That didn't happen either. When he covertly glanced over his shoulder it was to find that, apparently unable to voice any objections, she had begun following obediently behind him, her expression pensive and closed as she stared at the ground.

Hale opened the passenger door for her, and then began loading her things into the back of the Jeep. He'd rolled the canvas top of the Jeep back and fastened it, making the car convertible. He was still waiting for a verbal assault, some remark from Diane to remind him of his place.

Nothing.

He got behind the wheel, turned over the engine and shifted into Reverse.

"How was your flight?" he found himself asking as he backed out of the parking space.

"Fine."

"Good."

He shifted into Drive and headed out of town along the North Shore Road.

Like the old British colonies on other Caribbean islands, the traffic moved on the left. He concentrated on his driving as the road twisted and curved sharply upward and the road rose above Cruz Bay. The air became cooler and there was a breeze. Out of his peripheral vision Hale was aware of how it tousled Diane's hair, but she didn't seem to care, actually turning her face into the wind and sunshine. He knew when she glanced his way, casually, several times. He could almost hear her thinking, *I can handle this.*

"No one told me you were going to be here," Diane finally said.

She sounded more disappointed than hostile.

"I didn't have any real plans for the holidays. Your folks invited me at the last minute. They said they didn't think you were coming. You didn't last year."

She glanced away, over the spectacular vista of scattered islands, bays and cays in the Atlantic. Hale knew why she hadn't spent the holidays with her family but thought better of saying so. Everyone has a history. Baggage. Sore points. No one knew that better than himself.

"Who's at the house?"

"Half the Eastern Seaboard," he said dryly. But she didn't smile. "Adam, Eva, the kids. Your brother Simon's coming sometime this week. Bailey brought along a girl pal, Courtney. Me. You."

"You weren't kidding," Diane commented. "Where's everyone sleeping? The house is not that big."

"You know that as long as there's a piece of floor space and a cot or sleeping bag Eva will make it work. I think Eva said Simon opted to stay at a guesthouse.

Something about not wanting to cramp his social life."

"He can be something else," she murmured.

"Really? That reminds me of someone else." Hale said with a meaningful drawl. She didn't take the bait.

Silence fell but Hale was still on the alert. He was aware that Diane was being unusually civil toward him. They were actually having a conversation that had not, as yet, deteriorated into sarcasm, attitude and insults.

"What about you?" she asked, swaying in her seat as he shifted and took another of the sharp curves that challenged drivers.

"I'm staying on board the sloop."

"You're not staying at the house?"

He honestly couldn't tell if she was pleased or not.

"Like you said, the house is not that big. I figure, family first. All others get in line. I don't mind."

Her gaze remained on him for a while but Hale pretended he didn't notice. He knew that this moment, the drive with her from Cruz Bay without histrionics, was major. Bigger than major. How long was it going to last?

Hale slowed as they approached a turnoff on the right, the road suddenly narrow and steep. He shifted into second and the Jeep easily took the climb, bumping along over the mostly dirt surface.

"I wish I knew how to drive stick," Diane said.

"Do you? How come?"

"So I could tear up this hill as if I was clearing a road through the jungle."

He merely nodded to show his appreciation and understanding.

The Jeep crested the road as it wound to the left, to a small clearing that overlooked the island-dotted ocean.

To the right was a modest but airy house set on an angle about fifty feet above the ground. There were steps that switched back once, leading from the road up to the wide veranda deck and the entrance. Beneath the deck was a carport, which was generally used as a staging area for loading and unloading vehicles. Barely visible was a recessed second level consisting of two rooms and a bath. Hale knew Adam had added it when Bailey and Hayden were still children, so they'd each have their own room when in residence on the island. From the sea looking back and up the side of the hill, the house looked a little like a two-tiered cake.

Even before he'd turned off the engine what seemed like a mob of people, but was actually only five, suddenly appeared from various openings and doors of the house, rushing toward them with shouts of "Merry Christmas, Merry Christmas," mixed with squeals of welcome and delight.

Hale remained seated and watched the scene unfold. He smiled slightly in amusement and envy as the extended Maxwell family descended upon Diane, wrapping her in great enthusiastic bear hugs. Smothering her with kisses. Circling her with love and attention. Diane pushed her sunglasses to the top of her head and, with a big smile and a wide gaze, she welcomed it all. As when he'd first seen her on the dock at Cruz Bay, she was completely unselfconscious. And her response to her family was really beautiful to witness.

Eva, petite and dwarfed by even her own two children, was the first to receive a kiss and hug from Diane. The other things distinguishing her from the young people around her were her short salt-and-pepper hair and her narrow, fashionable eyeglasses. Bailey, who was sixteen and almost as tall as her brother and Diane, muscled her way in next. Hayden, eighteen, crowded in to make it a three-person hug. Diane beckoned to Courtney next. She was shy with glasses and a little overweight. Hale had been told that she and Bailey had been best friends since grade school. Adam towered over them all, the patriarch and indomitable leader.

Diane tried to answer all the questions at once, laughing and being interrupted and shaking her head helplessly because everyone was talking over each other. They all admired her new hairstyle, Hayden commenting that she looked pretty hot, Bailey immediately decided she wanted her hair cut the same way.

Hale took in the warm and noisy family reunion and there was a part of him that suddenly wondered if it was such a good idea for him to be here, imposing himself on this very open and public display of familial love.

He had so little experience with it himself.

He got out of the Jeep and removed Diane's luggage. And while the greeting continued, the noise level finally settling down, he walked away from the gathering toward the house.

"I'll take one of those."

Adam Maxwell grabbed the tote filled with gifts and swung Diane's other bag to his shoulder.

"Damn! What the devil is she carrying in here?" he asked in his deep booming voice.

He started up the steps and Hale was right behind him. He noticed, as he had on a number of occasions, that Adam certainly didn't move like a man of a certain age carrying something too heavy. In fact, Hale was pretty impressed that Diane's father remained a vigorous, physically dominate person, one not easily ignored or forgotten. In the last few years there was evidence of a bit of middle-aged spread, but Adam could still not be considered fat. Even a year or so shy of sixty, he didn't have many gray hairs.

Hale was grateful that, more than anything, it had been Adam's commanding presence, his straightforward talk combined with a few threats, that had pulled his butt out of the fire at a time when he thought he knew more than he did. Hale never had any trouble admitting to anyone who was interested that Adam Maxwell had saved his life.

"Diane said she wasn't coming, so she gets what's left of a place to sleep around here," Adam said.

He proceeded through the large open main room of the house to the back. There was a small sundeck off the kitchen to the right with a deep wooden awning overhang that protected the space from rain. It was, however, completely screened in. With a pull-out love seat and a storage trunk that served as a table, the deck passed very nicely as an open-air bedroom. Private and quiet with a view of the sea from one end, where the sun was already sinking toward the western horizon.

Hale and Adam put down the bags. Adam looked at him closely.

"So? How was she when you picked her up?"

Hale leaned against the door frame and removed his dark glasses. He shrugged. "She was surprised but cool about it."

Adam raised his brows. "No hissy fit? No dramatic scene?"

"Nope. As a matter of fact, we actually talked on the drive back. It was…pleasant. Different."

"I'll bet," Adam said dryly. He took a deep breath and spread his arms. "So. No need for me to mediate a truce?"

"Not as far as I can tell."

"It's early yet. Watch your back."

Hale chuckled. "Point taken."

"Well, then." Adam's tone was not so much fatalistic as resigned. "Let the games begin."

Diane, now changed into a pair of shorts and a gauzy top, returned to the living room. With the excitement of her arrival long over, no one paid any attention to her as she wandered aimlessly around the room in her bare feet, familiarizing herself with what was new or different since her last visit to St. John.

But she was equally curious about where Hale was, and her wandering gaze darted about until she realized he was with her father on the veranda, quietly talking against the background of a setting tropical sun. It was as if she needed to affirm that he had not been an apparition that afternoon, waiting for her on the dock at Cruz Bay. Then she needed to question why, upon realizing it was indeed him, she'd felt light-headed, a peculiar sensation of déjà vu and tongue-tied. And she didn't know yet how she felt about sharing the holidays with him.

Diane sat in one of the high-back wicker chairs as Eva entered from the kitchen.

"That has got to be one of the most original Christmas trees I've ever seen," Diane said, making reference to a rather bizarre leafless arrangement of driftwood and Christmas lights.

"Don't laugh," Eva warned as she put down a tray with frosty glasses of iced tea and lemonade. "It's not like we can get evergreen down here. We make do. Don't you remember the year your father jerry-rigged a tree out of wire coat hangers and we wrapped it in crepe paper?"

"Daddy tried to attach a star lamp on top…"

"And it kept falling over." Eva laughed in merriment with Diane as she sat in a wicker rocker adjacent to her stepdaughter.

Diane's good humor continued as she watched her half sister and brother, and Courtney, try to sort out the labeled gifts underneath the tree.

"Has Hayden made a decision about a college for next fall?"

"He wants to accept the offer from Brown. Duke is his second choice. We'll still talking about it."

"I can't believe how tall Bailey has gotten just since her last birthday," Diane said with some amazement. "And she's so pretty."

"I know. Adam goes into meltdown every time a boy even looks at her."

"He wasn't like that with me," Diane commented thoughtfully.

"Well, he didn't need to be, honey. You were more than capable of taking care of yourself. He never had to worry about anyone taking advantage of you. You would have 'drop-kicked him to the curb.'" Eva chuckled, quoting her son.

Diane merely nodded. She was reminded of the times she'd discouraged some overeager, testosterone-driven boy because he'd gotten overly familiar with her. Not because she was totally uninterested but because she was so afraid of disappointing her father. And then she'd been introduced to Hale Cameron.

It had been during spring break one year in D.C. at Adam and Eva's house where she'd come to visit for two weeks from her mother and stepfather's home outside of Boston. She'd heard about Hale for months before, how her father has taken on the court-appointed guardianship of him rather than see the teen succumb to the temptations of street life or the influence of an older brother already serving time. Then she didn't know what to make of someone like Hale. Street-smart and sullen, talking a language she didn't understand. She'd made no mystery of her feelings about him. He was not worth it. He was trouble. She was going to prove it… until she'd found herself alone with him…in the family room late one night…

"Mom, can we open gifts now?" Bailey asked, getting impatient.

Diane squirmed, her recollections having an unexpected affect.

Blinking away the memory of that long-ago night she turned her attention to the front veranda. The sky was tinted deep blue with touches of rose and yellow blending into a gorgeous sunset. Her father and Hale were sitting enjoying beers and each other's company. Of course she wondered what they were talking about.

Her?

"…dinner to be so late. So, let's get started, okay? Adam? You and Hale come on in here."

Eva reached for her hand and squeezed it. "Honey, I'm so glad you came. It wouldn't be Christmas without you."

Diane smiled faintly. "What did you do last year and the year before when I didn't come?"

"Missed you a lot. Hoped you're getting over what happened."

Diane didn't want to talk about it.

"I'm okay. Don't worry about me. I have noticed that there's something different about you, though."

Eva briefly averted her gaze. "I've lost a little weight."

"And I'm not too happy about it, either," Adam interrupted as he and Hale returned to the living room. "Tell her she doesn't need to lose weight," he said to Diane. "I'm happy with every square inch of what I married."

"Adam!" Eva admonished.

At just that moment of the affectionate exchange, Diane caught Hale's glance. Their gaze locked and then she turned away, feeling embarrassed. As if she'd been a voyeur to something private and endearing.

The three teens went into action, organizing the distribution of gifts. All Diane and the other adults had to do was wait to be served.

The next hour was a mixture of oohs and aaahs and exclamations of pleasure and satisfaction. There was lots of kissing and hugging as thanks were given for each gift. That was their tradition. Diane was aware that Hale was not left out, and he garnered his fair share of presents. She was more than surprised by the amount of genuine affection and regard with which he was held by her family.

It made Diane feel as if there were things about her own parents, her siblings, that she was not aware of. Things about Hale that she had not known or never accepted before. Such as the fact that he was almost one of the family, that he did seem to belong.

For probably the first time she was seriously curious about Hale's background, and his own family. She didn't even know if he had one, other than his brother whose life, she'd always known, had taken him down a different path.

"This is for you. It's from Hale," Hayden said as he handed her the medium-size box.

"For me?" Diane asked, confused. She glanced at

Hale but he was actually distracted, helping Courtney with the instructions for her new iPod touch.

The box had weight to it. She resisted the urge to shake it as one might do if suspecting an explosive device.

Both Eva and her father sat watching her as she began to peel away the wrapping paper. Since she hadn't expected Hale to actually be on St. John, let alone have a gift for her, Diane's mind was a total blank as to what it could be.

Suddenly, the room was very quiet and she realized that everyone was now waiting for the big reveal. She only frowned when she read the side of the box. Tom Tom ONE 125.

"That's pretty cool," Hayden said, taking the box out of her hands.

"That's mine," Diane said, quickly taking the box back.

Adam and Eva laughed. Hayden shrugged. Hale silently watched her.

"What is it?" she asked.

"A GPS system," Eva said. "You use it in your car to get from point A to point B. I have one and I love it."

"It even talks to you," Bailey added helpfully. "It tells you when to turn and how far away you are from a street or whatever. It's pretty cool."

Suddenly, Diane understood. She glanced at Hale who watched her with the most serious expression on his face. She gave him a self-effacing grimace.

"Cute. I'm sorry to say I probably should use one."

"You almost don't have to think for yourself anymore," Hayden said.

Diane made a face at him. *Smart ass*, she mouthed, but he only grinned back.

"So, where does this go in my car?" she asked, opening the box to pull out the contents, examining the parts.

"On the dashboard. I'll show you how it works, if you like."

She glanced at Hale as he casually made the offer. "Thanks."

"You forgot something," Bailey said officiously.

Diane sighed inwardly. She stood, with the GPS in hand, and stepped over the debris in the middle of the floor until she could reach Hale. Bending, she planted a quick and light kiss on his cheek. He showed no surprise and said nothing. But Hale moved unexpectedly. Slightly. Not away but to accommodate her gesture.

She was suddenly reminded of the polite kiss Hale had been forced to give her under the mistletoe in Ron Jeffrey's office. And the one later that evening, which had been prompted not by holiday cheer and goodwill to all men but by something more complex. She had not rejected him either time. This time, neither had he.

"Okay, dinner!"

With that boisterous command from Adam, the Christmas gift exchange was considered over and done with. Everyone was instantly hungry and ready to eat. Diane was spared any further reflection.

Except that she was seated next to Hale. Diane was grateful that any tension between them was lost in the overall cheerful and irreverent conversation and laughter of Christmas dinner. No one was spared teasing or embarrassing questions or unasked-for opinions or comments...like any other family.

Eva had prepared a feast of apricot-glazed fresh ham, mashed potatoes, vegetables and biscuits served family style, everyone helping themselves and each other.

While the kids cleaned up the mountains of torn and shredded gift-wrap paper, Diane helped Eva wrap and store leftovers in the kitchen. Hale took care of carting the garbage down to an outdoor bin and Adam cleared the table.

Turning from a cabinet stocked with plastic storage containers, Diane caught her father in the act of kissing his wife. It was a quick peck on the mouth. The action was spontaneous but so loving that Diane felt like she was somehow invading a very private moment. She turned quickly away only to see Hale crossing the living room from the veranda. Diane knew he must have witnessed the exchange between her father and Eva as well. Once again, she and Hale's gaze met before they both turned away.

Hale knelt to organize all the opened gifts under the tree so that there was room to move around. Diane distracted herself by helping with the gifts. They worked in silence, but conversation and laughter around them filled the house with background noise.

"I wasn't expecting anything from you," Diane finally said quietly.

"Of course not," he said smoothly, taking a box holding a sweater.

"That's not what I mean," she said quickly, defensively.

Hale sat back on his haunches and looked at her, amused. "Look. Let's agree to stop tap-dancing around each other. I won't second-guess you if you don't second-guess me. I'll say what I mean and you do the same, deal?"

She studied him for a long moment and silently nodded. He was being sincere. And he was right.

"I don't have anything for you," Diane admitted.

"Are you offering a rain check?"

"Do you want one?"

"Sure, why not? Might come in handy one day."

It was only ten o'clock when it became clear that everyone had pretty much had it for the day. The kids trekked off to the upper-level bedrooms. Eva got linens for Diane's bed and together they made up the love seat while once again Adam and Hale sat on the veranda in quiet conversation.

"What do they talk about?" Diane asked Eva.

"Everything," Eva said, sitting on top of the trunk as she watched Diane complete the making of the pull-out bed. "It's sacred ground, so to speak. I never hear much about what they discuss. I think it's good for Adam. He's not close to that many men. And it's very good for Hale. He respects Adam so much."

Diane took all of that in. She wanted very much to ask if her father and Hale ever talked about her. But why would they? She'd made it clear years ago that she wasn't interested in someone like Hale, what he said or did.

The admission made her suddenly very uncomfortable.

"Were you surprised to find him on St. John?"

"That's an understatement," Diane confessed wryly.

"Honey, I know how you feel, but your father and I were happy he said he'd come. Hale doesn't have what we'd call good family. It's been hard for him."

"Hayden and Bailey seem to like him a lot."

"They do. He's very patient with them. He's also a good influence."

"Oh."

Eva yawned. "I'm so tired. It was a nice day, wasn't it?"

Diane glanced at her stepmother. "Are you okay?"

Eva avoided her eyes. "The kids are high-energy and high-maintenance. They can wear anybody out."

"You know if Daddy hears you saying that, he'll have words with them."

"I know, and I don't want him to. I...it really has nothing to do with the kids." Eva got up to say good-night. She stroked Diane's arm in passing. "We'll talk tomorrow."

Diane considered Eva's comment, her mind rushing ahead as she tried to guess what was going on, if anything, with her stepmother. She was still mulling over possibilities when she went into the kitchen to fill a glass carafe with ice water for her room. She was aware that there was still someone on the veranda.

"Daddy?" Curious, she headed toward the open deck.

"It's Hale. I'm just leaving. Good night."

Diane pushed open the screen door and found him at the top of the steps. He was a large, looming shadow. She could make out the outline of his baseball cap and his wide shoulders under the light colored T-shirt. The shape of his athletic long legs that she knew were covered with little curls of dark hair. His face and expression were lost to her in the night.

"I guess we'll see you tomorrow."

He didn't answer right away, but Diane had the sense that he was watching her, or trying to in the dark.

"Probably. Merry Christmas, Diane." He started down the stairs.

"Hale," she called out, surprising herself. "I forgot

to thank you for the ride from Cruz Bay today. I was...I didn't expect to see you."

"I hope you're not going to let that spoil the holiday for you."

"I think I can handle it," she said lightly.

"Then you don't have to thank me. It's nice that you did." Hale started to leave and stopped again. "Look, I like taking a quick swim before calling it a night. Want to join me?"

"You mean right now? It's so late. It's dark."

"I know. You're not afraid, are you?"

Diane held her breath.

You're not afraid, are you?

That's exactly what he'd asked that night. A challenge. A dare.

"I'll get my things."

Chapter 5

Diane was a little surprised by how much traffic there was on the road into and out of town. Jeeps and SUVs and the big multiseat, open-air vans transporting groups of holiday vacationers to and from various activities. There were now dozens of restaurants, wine bars, cafés and clubs in Cruz Bay and Mongoose Junction, as well as the large chain hotels with their high-end amenities like large flat-screen TVs so they could host sports events and the latest Hollywood release on HD DVD.

The island had changed, Diane mused, since her first visits as a child in the years following her parents' divorce. She'd lived for the summers and flying to St. John to be with Adam. She'd first met Eva on a flight to the island. On St. John Eva had met Adam and here they'd fallen in love.

Diane remembered other times as well, like spring break from college, holidays or carnival when she didn't want to miss any of the local color. Those were the years of youthful indulgence, when hanging out with a group of friends or strangers provided excitement and instant gratification for the restlessness she sometimes felt.

Party like it's 1999.

She realized that the way she felt might be due to her parents' divorce and the feeling of having been abandoned, for a while, by both. Meeting Eva had changed her youthful outlook on her parents.

But Diane was glad that neither she nor Hale seemed inclined to that kind of entertainment tonight. Noise and endless drinking did not necessarily make for the most fun anymore. The idea of a nighttime swim with him sounded refreshing, enticing and…pretty romantic.

Who knew?

What she did know was that she was not about to pass this up. She just wasn't at all sure why.

After putting on a suit and grabbing a towel and a few other things she quietly left the dark house. Hale was waiting for her, the motor already idling. Diane was instantly reminded of another recent car ride with him that had led not only to revelations of truth, but to a catharsis that had given her several nights of dreams and fantasies. She was beginning to feel that way again.

The silence felt a little awkward and Diane asked questions as a way of dealing with it, not knowing what Hale might have actually been thinking. How did he like staying on the sloop? He loved it. He liked the quiet out on the water at night. The sense of safety. Did he ever go into town at night? Sometimes. Just to see what was going on. Listen to music and have a few beers.

Diane resisted the urge to ask if he'd met anyone interesting in town. If he had, she'd then wonder if he'd ever brought anyone back to the sloop to stay the night.

She decided she didn't need to know.

The air was warm and still. Katydids and crickets were a background chorus. After a few miles all that could be heard, as Hale turned off the Shore Road into a small parking lot under the overhang of sea grape trees, was the gentle lapping of water onto the sandy beach. He shut off the engine and turned off the lights and they were plunged into darkness. But it was a magical darkness, Diane noted right away.

Out in the bay were maybe a half dozen anchored small craft. Only two were in use, as far as she could tell. One was her father's sloop, *Paradise*. In the distance above the horizon the sky seemed dotted with lights that indicated homes or small businesses on nearby islands. Overhead a perfectly clear night revealed millions of stars.

"Do you have everything?" Hale asked.

"Yes," Diane answered, patting her canvas tote.

"The Zodiac is this way."

He walked slowly so that she could keep up through the sandy underbrush of shrub roots and old leaves. As soon as they both hit the sand they removed their shoes and continued barefoot. The Zodiac, the motor-operated launch that was used to ferry them from land to the sailboat, was on the shore.

Hale pushed it down the beach incline and into the water. He held the mooring line to keep it from drifting away. Having sailed with her father countless times as a child, Diane knew the routine. She put her things on the floor of the boat and carefully climbed in and took a seat near the bow. Hale pushed the launch into deeper water before getting in himself, sitting in the stern next to the throttle for the motor. They were soon moving soundlessly through the inky water toward the *Paradise*. The ride took all of thirty seconds.

The stairs leading up from the water and onto the deck were off the back. Again as Hale steadied the small craft, Diane got her footing and quickly climbed on board. Hale tied off the line and soon followed.

She walked the deck toward the bow, holding on to the cables and lines for balance. Behind her she could hear Hale. When she faced him he was in the process of peeling off his shirt. He stepped out of a pair of shoes as he unbuttoned his cargo shorts and removed them.

Diane tried not to look too long or to stare. His simple activity seemed provocative. Seeing Hale with so little on had an immediate effect. She felt suddenly vulnerable but also very female. She was aware of the physical differences between them covered by the merest bit of cloth. She felt hypnotized, watching Hale in his swimsuit. Not those godawful long jammers that reached almost to the knees or the baggy trunks like the ballplayers wore. Just simple, plain navy blue athletic shorts.

Her imagination ran rampant, mixed with a distinct memory. And for reasons she didn't care to look at too closely, Diane felt a little afraid.

She put down her bag and slowly began to undress as well. She removed her own peasant blouse and shorts to reveal her bikini, belatedly wishing that she'd worn a one-piece suit instead.

Was the suit too small? Too revealing? What if her body didn't do it justice?

Overwhelmed with doubts, she stepped onto the rail of the boat and jumped.

The water hit her hard, rushing up against her as she

plunged through the surface. Water saturated her hair. Unfortunately, the sheer force of the jump caused the top of her bikini to rip above her breasts and over her head.

Diane surfaced, gasping and sputtering with annoyance. She tried to tread water and cover her breasts at the same time, kicking to turn about in a futile search for the bikini top. She heard a splash nearby. The water displacement was much smaller and neater, and Hale surfaced within four feet of her.

"What was that all about? You okay?"

"No! I...lost my top!"

"What?"

"My *top*! I jumped in and it came right off! I can't find it."

If she was expecting sympathy or immediate offers to swim about and find the missing half of her suit, Diane was about to be severely disappointed.

Hale began to laugh.

Not a chuckle of amusement or a chortle of understanding but a deep, from-the-belly, laugh-out-loud bark that carried on the air through the dark.

"Stop it, Hale! This isn't funny," she hissed, frantic.

The laugh grew stronger. He went onto his back to float and continued to laugh with abandon.

Diane shoved her hand flat on the surface and a great wave of water splashed over Hale's face. It made no difference.

Helpless, Diane listened to him. She finally realized that he wasn't laughing at her. The humor of what had happened slowly occurred to her. It was funny. But she wasn't about to laugh and let him off the hook. She turned and began breaststroking away from him and the *Paradise*.

Hale gained control and called out after her.

"Hey! Where do you think you're going?"

"Why do you care?" she answered, and kept going toward the opening of the bay.

Diane went several strokes further but now there was no sound behind her at all. She stopped and flipped over, looking back. She could see the sailboat and the lights from St. John in the background. She couldn't see Hale.

"Hale!" she called.

Nothing.

"If you're trying to scare me it won't work."

Nothing.

"Hale?"

She turned and treaded, and paddled and treaded.

"Hale? Don't do this. I'm..."

Something grabbed her ankle and yanked. Diane squealed instantly in genuine fright and began kicking defensively, her heart racing. And then there was a sudden geyser of water in front of her. She squealed again. Hale broke the surface and hooked an arm around her waist. Diane felt herself being hauled, lifesaving fashion, back to the *Paradise*.

"What are you doing? Let me go!"

They reached the hull of the boat and he released her.

"You need to be tied and gagged," he said sternly. "You need to have your butt whipped. You just need to get over yourself and grow up. You don't need the top. Nothing to see anyway. Your vanity is safe."

With that he swam away from her, easily and smoothly, but more or less around the boat, keeping it within reach. Diane watched him and came to her senses. He was right. She'd acted foolishly. Childishly. Again. They weren't teenagers anymore.

Hale was the only man she'd ever known who wouldn't put up with her tantrums or her games. The only one who never hesitated to put her in her place when it was called for.

And he'd also never belittled her, although God knows there were times when he was within his rights to.

Properly chastised, she treaded water in place and swallowed some of her pride. She began to breaststroke again, slowly and comfortably, counting to herself until she found her rhythm. Finally she began to relax and enjoy the pure pleasure of suspension in the cool dark water.

She followed behind Hale but kept a distance. His presence became comforting. She experienced a sense of peace and order and safety. It was a surprise to her, something she realized she hadn't known, had not even allowed herself, in nearly two years. The awful weight of guilt, embarrassment of those two years and a failed marriage, felt like it was being washed away.

She stopped swimming and pushed herself into a floating position. Gently sculling with her arms to stay in place, she turned her face upward. She could feel her wet hair floating around her face.

"What do you see?"

Hale was close again, floating next to her.

"I see…diamonds in the sky."

"Never could see this in D.C. where I came from."

She waited. He'd never made reference to his past before. At least, not to her.

"When I was a little girl I thought there were only

stars down here, over St. John. That's why I always felt this was a special place."

"Sure is."

They were quiet for a long time, just enjoying the night, the quiet. Then Diane began to feel chilled in the water, her fingers already pruney and slightly wrinkled.

"Ready to get back on board?" Hale asked.

She was relieved that he'd read her mind.

"Okay."

They reached the steps and Hale climbed aboard first. Diane was peeved that he didn't let her go ahead. But when she reached the top of the steps Hale was standing behind a towel held up for her. Murmuring a thank-you, she turned her back to him and took the towel ends to wrap and twist around her wet body sarong fashion.

Hale had toweled off and gone below deck, leaving Diane alone. She sat on the built-in bench at the stern. Finding another stack of towels, she used a second one to tie around her wet hair like a turban. When Hale came back he was carrying a can of beer for himself and a soda for her.

"Thanks," she said, accepting the frosty can and popping the tab to sip. She hugged the towel to her body with her arms, aware that she was mostly naked beneath it.

"I have wine, if you'd like that instead."

"This is fine," she said, lifting her soda can briefly.

Hale seemed to be studying the beer can with deep intent and fell silent. Diane had the feeling that, as had been the case since they'd first seen each other weeks earlier, he wasn't going to start and lead any conversation. It was up to her.

"Where is your family?"

Hale's head snapped up, his expression first surprised and then wary.

"Why do you want to know?"

She shrugged, sipping from the soda. "Curious. Everyone has family. It seems strange that you're not with them for the holidays. I never hear anything about yours."

He arched a brow and a sardonic grin lifted a corner of his mouth. "I've been told you're not interested and could care less. I believe that's a direct quote."

Her gaze dropped and she fiddled with her terry cloth turban. "My father told you, didn't he? I...did say that once. It was a long time ago."

"I don't know if all that much has changed, Diane."

He said it easily with no rancor or anger. Just a statement of fact. It hit a nerve.

"That's not true."

He glanced sharply at her again.

"When I saw you at that gala that night, I...I wasn't expecting to see you so I..."

"You shot from the hips," he said dryly.

She nodded. "You're right. And later driving home, I realized I'd behaved very badly. Childishly. Like...just like when I was seventeen. I felt terrible."

He sat perfectly still watching her, not responding and not reacting.

"I really did," she said earnestly. "Frankly, I surprised myself. Why did I do that?"

"I know why."

"Tell me," she pleaded, more eagerly than she realized.

Hale continued to study her and then slowly shook his head. "I think you know. Or you'll soon figure it out."

Diane was disappointed and frustrated. She gnawed on her lip and shrugged. "I guess I deserved that."

"Deserve is not the point."

Silence fell between them as they finished the cold drinks. Hale frowned at his empty can.

"My family, such as it is, saw a lot of hard times when I was growing up. I can't really remember when we weren't struggling to pay rent or buy food, or do anything. My father couldn't hold a job. He didn't like taking orders from anybody. He'd get mad at being criticized or asked to do something he didn't want to do and quit. He never stayed anyplace more than a month or two."

Now it was Diane's turn to sit perfectly still. She listened, fully aware that he was making a huge concession. After all, she knew she had no right to expect him to explain his life or background but she didn't want him to stop.

"He and my mom fought all the time. Over money, him not working, other women, his low-life friends. Everything was always somebody else's fault for my father. He was found dead in a deserted lot not far when where we lived. Never found out why or who did it. Then my brother started acting like him. Dropped out of school, ran the streets, went after the easy money. He got a girl pregnant. Then another.

"One night, he was with the wrong people in the wrong place at the wrong time. Someone ended up dead. Was he responsible? Don't know. But he was there, an accessory after the fact. He was nineteen at the time. Now he's doing fifteen to twenty-five for second-degree murder."

Hale's recitation was precise and matter-of-fact. His tone was almost flat, like he'd told this story before and the details never changed. He knew it all by heart. Underneath, however, Diane could hear not only despair but disappointment. She could sense, as surely as Hale continued to feel, the utter waste of it all. But she didn't know any of this when they were teenagers. And she'd known nothing about benefit of the doubt. Or second chances.

"What happened to your mother?"

He sighed, shifted positions. "My mother started drinking, maybe to dull her pain and frustration and helplessness. She tried to keep my brother and me on track. Didn't work for him. Pretty much didn't work for me either at first. She died when I was sixteen. Not from drinking. I was told she had a blood clot."

"Did she smoke?"

He shook his head.

"Was she diabetic? Have high blood pressure?" She asked, the physician in her rising.

"Diabetes for sure," Hale acknowledged. "And trouble with her cholesterol."

"Both are very possible causes, Hale."

He was pensive for a second, as if processing this confirmation. He was trusting her word as a doctor.

"So what happened after she died?"

"I went to live with my grandmother. Then she died. I ended up with an aunt, my father's sister. She got a new man and I had to leave. She put me out."

Diane closed her eyes and tried to shield her expression of disbelief. She'd had no idea.

"I moved in with a friend. I had no place else to go. I got caught with him and some other guys for trying to hijack a truck with a shipment of computers. I landed in jail for grand theft, and then in front of a judge. My life as I'd known it ended that day. It began again when I met Adam."

She waited for him to continue. Diane frowned when he got up and began picking up the wet towels, putting things away.

"Then what happened?" she asked, impatient to know more.

"That's it. Story time is over. I have to take you back."

"Wait, please. I know Daddy was a court-appointed guardian. How did that happen? He never said."

Hale raised a sardonic brow. "And you never asked?"

She stared at him. "No."

He pursed his mouth and shrugged. "My court lawyer knew Adam. He said all I needed was a strong hand and a good role model. He had the charges against me reduced, and Adam said, yeah, he'd take me on. He laid down the ground rules. I knew better than to cross him or to mess up."

Hale was staring at her, his eyes filled with a realization she didn't fully understand.

"Best thing that ever happened to me."

It was clear after that he wasn't going to continue. Reluctantly Diane got up and gathered her things. While Hale made sure the deck was clear of any obstruction, she replaced her sarong with her original blouse, satisfied that she was sufficiently covered for the drive back to the house. The ride in the Zodiac seemed even shorter going back to shore. She realized that, in a way, she didn't want the night to end. There was something about it, about the time on the *Paradise* with Hale, that seemed oddly perfect.

The roads were now deserted. There was only so

much to do at night on St. John, and island life generally shut down by midnight.

And there was no need for conversation. Hale had revealed enough to keep her mind busy, with only perfunctory questions or comments between them. Just before Hale reached the turnoff to the house, Diane touched his arm.

"Let me off here."

He stopped the Jeep. "I'll take you to the top of the drive."

"No, don't. The car engine might wake someone. Noise carries here. There's a makeshift staircase just next to that shrub over there. I'll take that. It's probably quicker." She began to climb out of the Jeep.

He held her arm. "I don't like leaving you down here."

She smiled at him in the dark, pleased with his concern. "I'll be fine. I've taken the path hundreds of times. I'll throw down a rock or something so you know I reached the end of the driveway."

"Just don't drop it on my head."

She chuckled.

He reached under his seat and pulled out a small plastic bag and handed it to her. "Take this with you."

"What is it?" She fingered the bag.

"You forgot it on the boat."

Hale sat waiting for her to get out. Instead, Diane swiveled in her seat to face him.

"I have one more question."

The humming engine was the only sound until finally he spoke.

"Go ahead."

"That night after you took me to see Jenna and her new baby...why did you kiss me that way?"

He sighed and played with the steering wheel, turning it back and forth. "I've thought about it. I don't really know. It just happened."

"Know what I think?"

"I'm afraid to ask," he murmured dryly.

"I think you just wanted to kiss me."

He chortled. "Still so sure of yourself."

"No, I'm not. That's why I asked."

Diane got out and walked around to his side.

"Know what else? Maybe I wanted you to kiss me."

It was not so dark that she couldn't detect the disbelief in his eyes. The frown on his brow.

And then she kissed *him*.

She only meant to touch his mouth, to leave a light peck with the pursing of her lips. But having come this far it really seemed pointless to not take full advantage. Hale made it easy for her. As she withdrew for a hesitant moment, he pursued her, leaning forward just enough to capture her mouth. He didn't have to force it open, Diane did that all on her own.

The kiss had a slow eroticism to it, as their tongues played and danced, as their mouths worked together. It really felt to Diane like they were doing this together, at the same pace, with the same caution and with the same results.

Hale laid his hand briefly along the side of her face, slid it down to place his thumb on her chin to control the tilt of her head, the pressure of his lips. She began to feel languid. Soft and giving. He placed his hands on her waist and gently but firmly pushed her away.

"Hale…"

"Good night, Diane. Go home."

"But I…"

"What?"

"I wanted to say about tonight…it was the best Christmas gift."

He sat quietly for a second, and then shifted gears to Reverse.

"You're welcome."

Diane turned quickly away and began the climb up the hidden steps, even in the dark running most of the way. She came to the top and, kicking her sandaled feet through some of the dirt, located a rock for her purpose. Carefully, she aimed it over the ledge and tossed it. It thudded on the ground. A second later she could hear Hale make a U-turn on the road and head back in the direction of Cruz Bay.

At the stairs leading up to the house she removed her sandals and continued barefoot to the veranda, through the kitchen to the back room. Within minutes she was in bed, reliving the evening, smiling in the dark over the lighthearted moments, pleased that there *were* lighthearted moments. Wiggling in the bed as she recalled the parting kiss.

Suddenly, Diane's eyes popped open and she sat up in bed, reaching for her tote. She pulled out the plastic bag Hale had given her. She opened it and found her damp bikini top inside.

It was the second time she'd had a dream about Hale in a week. This one was different.

She was sunbathing on the veranda, stretched out on her back on a chaise lounge, naked… Her eyes were closed, and she could hear the ocean. She was waiting, feeling the sun heat her skin. She was waiting and felt dreamy and soft with anticipation. A shadow appeared above her and she didn't have to open her eyes to know

*who it was. She sighed in relief. He cupped a breast
and squeezed her nipple, caressed her body making
her writhe. He lay atop her, his body heavy and hot
and hard. He pressed against her so she could feel the
stiff length of him, kissing her so that she didn't want
him to stop. She waited like she'd waited her whole life
for the touch of him, to ease the ache. He ground their
hips together. She moaned, wanting him to touch her
there. She'd do anything to make that feeling last....*

This time when she woke up it was already dawn.
She lay listening to early morning and the quiet of the
house. She was damp, like several mornings ago, but
only in one part of her body. She felt restless but now
she knew what she was dealing with.

Diane closed her eyes and languished in the stillness.
But she did not feel calm or peace, just resolve. Just very
agitated in a very specific way, in a very particular place.
She rolled onto her back again. She was so glad she'd
changed her mind about coming to St. John.

Chapter 6

Diane stood silently in the doorway that led out to the open veranda. Only Eva was on the deck, sitting in the shade of a potted plant and staring pensively out to sea. On her lap was an open magazine.

"Looks like another perfect day," she murmured. Eva started.

"You're up! How'd you sleep?"

"Like a baby. What time is it?" Diane asked, padding barefoot onto the veranda. She squinted out to the water where the bright sunlight reflected like bits of crystal on the surface.

Eva smiled at her. "It's a little after eleven. Does it really matter? You're on vacation."

Diane sighed, made a futile attempt to finger comb her matted hair and plunked herself down onto a canvas deck chair. She stretched like a cat.

"I never sleep this late."

"Frankly, you looked like you could use some rest when you arrived yesterday. Want something to eat?"

"Not yet. I want to shower and do something with my hair."

Eva frowned at her. "What happened to it?"

"Oh…I got sweaty in the night," Diane murmured, thinking fast. "I sleep all over the bed, so I guess I look a mess." She looked around. "Where is everybody?" She resisted the urge to walk to the end of the driveway and glance down the rise to see if Hale's Jeep was parked below.

"Everybody's out with Adam, sailing. Hayden is getting good at piloting the boat, but no way is your father going to trust him out alone yet."

"Who's everybody?"

"You know. Everybody," Eva said with a gesture. "The kids and Hale. Bailey wanted to wake you but Hayden and Adam were impatient to get started. Like father, like son."

"When did they leave? I didn't hear a thing."

"About eight."

"Oh, my God. That's obscene," Diane groaned.

"So, you're stuck with me."

Diane smiled warmly at her stepmother. "I would say we finally have some quality time alone."

"That means you want to gossip about everything and everyone."

"Yes," Diane confirmed. "But not until I shower and put some clothes on."

With that she sprang up and headed back inside. She was anxious to have a good chat with Eva, but Diane was immediately preoccupied with her experience of the night before and an erotic dream that seemed more and more prophetic. She was, to put it simply, hot and bothered and breathless. And if not for these damned dreams she'd been having almost every night, then a swim with Hale and a tantalizing parting kiss might be enough.

In the shower the cool water and soap seemed to slough off their past. In its place Diane imagined fresh possibilities. She was sorry she'd missed the chance to sail with her father and siblings, but recognized that maybe it was just as well. She needed some time to figure out what was going on between her and Hale.

Diane dressed in a pair of linen capri pants and a pale orange tank top. She let her hair air dry and made a headband out of a scarf to tie around it. In the kitchen she filled a small plate with a selection of fruit and finished off what was left of coffee in the maker. Then she rejoined Eva on the veranda.

For a while their conversation was just a catch-up of family news over the past few months. Eva laughing relating Adam's annoyance that Diane had turned over his award check after the gala in Baltimore to the grant foundation...without asking him. Hayden was starting college in eight months and would be leaving home. Bailey would graduate high school the year after.

And with talk of children came the understandable reflection about Gail, Eva's child from her first marriage. Eva's daughter and husband had died tragically in a house fire. With equanimity she remarked that Gail would be twenty-six now, had she lived.

Diane briefly squeezed her stepmother's hand, but then rushed on to another subject that she knew would return Eva's smile.

"What about Daddy?"

"Oh, you know your father. If your question is when is he going to retire, the answer is never. And I'm just as happy, to be honest. He's so high-energy that if he had nothing to do he'd drive me crazy in no time.

"He's been asked to teach graduate courses at Howard, and I believe the Naval Academy would like to make him a visiting professor for a year. He can teach whatever he wants."

"That's great," Diane said with a grin.

She wasn't the least bit surprised. A former marine biologist, her father had been the only African American in the field for years. That alone had brought him to national attention when she herself was still a child.

"And what about Hale?"

Eva slowly turned a surprise countenance to her. "Excuse me? Did you just ask about Hale?"

"Yes, I did."

"Why?"

"What do you mean, why? He's practically a member of the family. What's he been up to?"

Eva stared at her, her mouth opened in shock. And then she pulled herself together, her expression changing to curiosity and skepticism.

"I'm sorry, but you're not going to get away with that offhand attitude. When you were sixteen and seventeen you treated that poor boy like dirt. Even as you grew older you were very hard on him, Diane. What's going on?"

Diane knew it was futile to pretend that she'd never harbored ill will toward Hale. She sighed.

"Maybe it was seeing him here yesterday, being part of our Christmas and…fitting in. One of the things I noticed was he doesn't seem to take his relationship with you and Daddy for granted."

"He doesn't," Eva said emphatically. "It took years of talking and cajoling to convince Hale that he was always welcomed with us. *Always*. I'm sorry you never gave him a chance when he was a teenager."

"You're defending him," Diane said with surprise.

"Yes, I am. But he doesn't need me to. Hale's actions have always spoken better about him than his past."

Diane frowned. She knew that.

"What have you two been talking about?"

Diane hesitated. She wasn't sure how much she should reveal yet. It all seemed so unformed. She and Hale were still scratching around in the dark, still circling each other cautiously.

"I wanted to know about his family. What he told me was…pretty sad."

"And not so unusual for a lot of young black boys. Hale got lucky, and he knows it."

"I know. He told me as much."

"To be honest, at the time I was surprised that Adam let himself be talked into being a court-appointed guardian by Judge Norman Oliver. Judge Oliver used to live a few doors down from us, remember? So now you two are talking. What does that mean, exactly?"

Diane had the feeling that there was a double meaning in Eva's question. She answered the easy part.

"It means that we're being civil and getting to know each other better. It means now that we're grown up we have more in common."

She wasn't sure she was ready to confess how much she liked him. How much she felt physically drawn to him. Like when she was seventeen and so naive.

"Honey, it would have happened a lot sooner if you hadn't been so hard on Hale."

"Maybe," Diane murmured, knowing full well the story was not so simple.

As much as she'd resented Hale's place in her father's

life, feeling as if he was siphoning off attention she didn't want to share, there was that confusing awareness of him as being so different from other boys. He wasn't a boy, but closer to being a man. He wasn't polite or cajoling or flirtatious. He didn't try seduction to get into her pants. If anything at all, he'd been indifferent to her. And that enraged her. Who did he think he was? Some punk thug from the hood who should be grateful he'd been taken in?

Hale ignoring her made her feel Hale didn't think she was pretty or sexy. Until that night when her parents were out and she and Hale were alone. Diane drew in her breath with the recollection of how she'd teased him and manipulated him into…

"He's…a lawyer?" Diane asked, clearing her throat when her voice cracked.

"He is," Eva said proudly. "Started out as an assistant D.A., but switched when he had an opportunity to go corporate. Hale didn't have all the advantages you did, but he's a good man."

Diane all but cringed. That's what Jenna had said.

"Okay, okay. So he walks on water."

Eva laughed. Diane used it as a means of switching topics.

"Want to tell me what's going on with you?"

Eva's humor died quickly. She looked out to sea. "Oh…I don't know. Maybe I'm overreacting."

"Why don't you tell me what's bothering you and let me decide if you're overreacting. That's why you hinted yesterday that not all was well. It's not you and Daddy, is it?"

Eva looked genuinely surprised, and then her expression softened and her lashes actually fluttered. She seemed embarrassed by her own thoughts.

"No. Oh, no. We're…Adam and I…well…"

"So you're not having any marital or sexual problems."

Eva couldn't seem to respond, the topic was so suddenly personal. She simply closed her eyes and shook her head.

Diane smiled to herself. She was ten years old when she'd first met Eva, on a flight down to St. John as it happened. She knew it must be a little odd for Eva to have her grown-up stepdaughter—even if she was a doctor—make reference to her intimate life.

"Are you in pain? Uncomfortable in some way?"

Eva seemed relieved to be directed toward the possibilities.

"Sometimes I get cramps in my stomach. Below my navel. And in my lower back at the same time. Sometimes when Adam and I…afterward, I hurt a little."

Diane listened carefully and gave Eva her full attention, seeing that her stepmother, who barely looked more than forty, was going through something real. She nodded, mentally cataloging the complaints. And in a way that surprised her, she was so glad that as a doctor she could help someone she loved so much.

"I feel bloated. Adam's been teasing me that I'm either pregnant or getting fat."

Although she said it with a caustic grin Diane could hear the uncertainty beneath the attempt at humor.

"Glad he can joke about it. I'll have to have some words with him about *his* pouch. I'll be right back."

Diane returned to her room and rummaged through her luggage until she found the case with her stethoscope and blood pressure kit. Eva didn't seem the least bit surprised that medical equipment was among her vacation gear. Diane told her she never went away anywhere without these basic tools of her profession.

"I'm just going to take some preliminary readings and, if you don't mind, I'll like to look at your stomach."

Diane was glad that her stepmother could joke, even uneasily, about the sofa doubling very nicely as an examination table. It didn't take long and when she was done she gave Eva a quick hug and kiss on the cheek.

"Don't worry. Gynecology is not my area but if I'm right I don't think it's serious. Worst case, it's endometriosis. But it's more likely cysts. They're generally harmless little bubbles that attach to either the uterus or ovaries. They can get big, creating pressure and pain in the pelvic area. Have you been bleeding heavier than usual?"

Eva nodded.

"Well, I'll get you something to help with the pain, but I'd like you to get an ultrasound."

Diane began to put her things away and was curious when Eva grabbed her hand.

"Please don't tell your father."

"It's nothing serious, I'm sure."

"I know, but…Adam will worry more than he needs to, and…"

"You mean he's overprotective."

Again, Eva nodded.

"That's…very sweet," Diane said, squeezing Eva's hand. "Okay. I won't say anything. If you're taking any medications I'd like to see what they are."

"Just a few. I'll get them for you."

Eva sat adjusting her clothing and Diane returned to her room and put her tools on the bed. Then she sat on the edge thinking about her parents. Thinking about herself and Trevor.

As a matter of fact, to her way of thinking, her father and Eva's was a rare relationship. Adam Maxwell didn't just love his second wife, he adored her. And yes, he was protective.

Diane used to think it was because Eva was so small, so petite and delicate physically. However, Eva was probably the one person on the face of the earth who was capable, fearlessly, of putting Adam Maxwell in his place when it was needed. Diane smiled ruefully. Even she, his eldest child, didn't have that kind of power.

As a teenager she'd been outright jealous of their closeness and wondered if her father's second family, with the birth of Hayden and then Bailey, would push her to the background. She'd already achieved that status with her natural mother's second marriage and the birth of Simon. And, of course, it had surfaced with a vengeance when Hale entered the scene. But Eva had comfortably, without effort or pretense, always made sure that her place in her father's life was secure, along with his love and regard.

It was only when her father had made himself responsible for Hale Cameron that she'd again felt vulnerable…and unwanted. He was not family, and that had made it easy for her to belittle him, to treat him as an interloper and resent having to share him with her parents. Even as Hale had the ability to get her excited.

Diane also recognized, now that she'd attempted and failed at her own brief marriage, that what she wanted was exactly what her father had achieved with marrying Eva. Someone who loved him, and whom he loved, unconditionally. Someone who was so thoroughly the right person for him. Adam had once said so himself, confiding in her when she was fourteen or fifteen that he didn't know how he'd gotten so lucky as when he'd met Eva Duncan that summer on St. John.

"This is what I've been taking." Eva suddenly appeared, thrusting a handful of pharmacy bottles at her. "They're back," Eva quickly added before rushing off to greet her returning family.

But Diane continued to sit. She absently looked at the individual labels. Mostly vitamin supplements. One or two were unnecessary, she thought, and made a note to tell Eva so. One bottle was a hormone replacement and another for high blood pressure. She frowned at these, as well, questioning the need for the prescriptions.

The arrival of the family filled the house with life. She put the medication bottles on the bed next to her. She was feeling a sudden terrible loneliness. Even a gripping fear, that maybe she just wasn't the kind of woman that men wanted to love. Or cherish. "Til death do they part."

And why not?

The sudden queasiness in her stomach signaled she understood more than she was willing to admit.

It sounded like a small army had arrived in the driveway below. She heard her father's booming voice, telling Hayden and Bailey to go rinse off the snorkeling equipment and asking Courtney to take the picnic basket up to the kitchen. She heard Eva going out to the veranda to wait for them, knowing she would greet each one with an affectionate kiss.

Her father and Eva had never been shy about that. Showing how they felt about one another.

Finally Diane roused herself from her contemplative stupor to go and say hello. Plus to see if Hale had returned to the house with them as well.

* * *

Hale had learned long ago to stay out of the way of the Maxwell family when they were all together in the same place. He lurked in the background, trying not to be obtrusive. Sometimes it was hard to be an inadvertent witness to their open affection for each other.

He felt like a voyeur.

Hale trailed behind, as he often did, until everyone had settled down, and his presence simply became an accepted fact. But this time was different. There was the added awareness of Diane. Ever since Adam had gotten under sail out of the small marina at Chocolate Hole, he'd been thinking about her and wondering what she was doing. But to be honest, Hale was not disappointed that she had not joined them. It was no longer possible to keep up any pretense that they were nothing to each other. Since the moment he'd met her on the dock in Cruz Bay, he'd recognized that their youthful animosity toward each other had mysteriously become serious adult attraction.

He didn't see her right away and thought perhaps she'd gone out somewhere on her own for the day.

He didn't know if what he felt just then was disappointment or relief.

And then she did suddenly appear, coming into the living room quietly and unobserved by everyone except him. She glanced openly at him for a moment, on her silent journey around the boisterous cluster of her family. He pretended not to see her. She seemed to be headed toward him.

Hale felt a genuine moment of panic. Their little adventure the night before was still fresh enough in his memory that he was afraid he'd give something away, either to Diane or to her family. He feigned a distraction by chatting briefly with Courtney to find out how she'd enjoyed her first attempt at snorkeling. When he turned, Diane was standing close to his side.

He could smell her.

She'd showered earlier with some botanically scented soap. Her hair was simply but attractively tied with a banded scarf. She looked barely older than Bailey. Still as young as when they'd…

"Hi. How was the sail?" she asked.

She was standing too close. It made him…too aware of her.

"Pretty nice. We headed over to Jost Van Dyke to swim. Had lunch there."

"Sorry I missed it," she murmured, looking at her bare feet.

"Maybe just as well. Being around teenagers is an interesting experience," he commented. "It's all about *them*."

Diane smiled rather coyly at him. "Don't forget, we were once teenagers."

Hale made a point of catching her gaze and holding it.

"Yes. I remember very well."

He had the satisfaction of seeing her almost blush.

"What did you two do while we were gone?" Adam asked Eva and Diane as he sat himself in a chair and propped his feet on the coffee table.

Neither answered right away. Curious, Hale observed the two women exchange covert glances.

"It was a girl thing," Diane responded lightly. Her father laughed.

"We talked and talked," Eva said with a shrug.

"And talked some more," Diane reiterated.

"Don't act like you even missed us." Eva chortled.

"It would have been nice to have you along," Adam admitted, speaking in a warm tone that Hale knew was for his wife.

Hale felt like he would give anything to know how it was done. How do you love someone *that* much? How do you build the trust? How long is it supposed to take?

"I couldn't leave Diane alone," Eva explained, "since no one else volunteered to stay and keep her company."

"I didn't realize there was an option," Hale found himself saying quietly.

"She's a big girl. I'm sure she's used to being alone."

Hale watched as Diane visibly cringed at her father's thoughtless remark. Even Eva swatted her husband on his shoulder to silently chastise him. Hale walked over to the stack of gifts under the tree and searched until he located a box. He stood and turned to Diane.

"Come on. You and I are going out for a while." He headed to the veranda.

"We are?" Diane asked, caught off guard.

"You are?" Adam and Eva said together.

"Can we come?" Bailey asked, pulling Courtney next to her.

"'Fraid not," Hale said emphatically. He held up the box. "I'm going to show Diane how to use her GPS system."

"Oh…" Bailey grimaced, losing all interest in accompanying them.

"Besides, you're both sandy and your hair's wrecked. Go shower. Both of you. You too, Hayden. I'll make some snacks," Eva said, getting up and heading into the kitchen.

Hale could have kissed her.

He looked at Diane. Her eyes were bright and regarded him with smiling consideration.

"Let's go," he said smoothly and she followed him down the stairs to the front of the yard.

"Where's your Jeep?" she asked him.

Hale began removing the contents of the box. He gave her the instruction booklet and told her to put it away somewhere safe, just in case.

"Still down at the bay. I caught a ride back here with Adam."

"But I can't drive stick," she reminded him.

"You will. I'm going to show you on Adam's car for now. Get in," he said, already climbing behind the wheel.

Diane did so. Hale thought for sure she'd be a little annoyed. If not by the insult of her needing a guidance system in her car, then at least by the idea of him teaching her a thing or two about driving. He was surprised to see that she seemed willing and enthusiastic.

He backed up to turn around to descend the steep driveway.

"Hey!"

Hale hit his breaks sharply as Adam's voice grabbed their attention from the veranda above.

"Simon will probably be on the four o'clock ferry. Pick him up, will you?"

With a wave from Diane, Hale continued down to the paved main road.

"We're going to the street behind the school yard, just outside of Great Cruz Bay," Hale announced, expertly shifting as he took the curvy turns. "It should be deserted because of the holidays. We'll let you practice there. Then I'll show you how to use the GPS."

"Hale?"

He gave her a quick glance, not taking his eyes from the road for more than a second.

"Pull over."

"Why?"

"Just do it."

Although confused, and suspicious, Hale did as asked, driving onto a shoulder of the road so narrow that the Jeep was tilted at an angle.

He turned to look at Diane askance. Before he could do anything else, Diane had leaned toward him, curved her hand around the side of his head and began kissing him.

He wasn't going to respond as if he were a trained pet for her amusement. But the instant he felt the soft searching of her mouth, the persistence with which Diane sought to share her tongue with him, he caved in.

He was not happy with how easy it had been. But God, she tasted good.

He hated the thought that she had won after all.

Hale gave as good as he got, and didn't deny that kissing in this deeply intimate way was having its affects. A taxi van rattled by and the passengers, spotting him and Diane in the middle of nonverbal communication, whistled and hooted and cheered them on.

It was enough of a distraction to get his attention. He pulled away.

"What do you think you're doing?" he asked, hoping his voice was sufficiently firm.

She smiled seductively at him, her eyes bright but hooded. "Couldn't you tell?"

"Why now?" he asked, more softly.

"Why not? Isn't it about time?"

He couldn't respond. That was his thought exactly.

"I'm apologizing. I'm admitting that I was a little bitch to you. I was a tease, and impossible, and I was very young. And...I was wrong."

He gazed into her eyes wide with earnestness and, much to his surprise and reluctant admiration, he believed her.

She was nothing if not fearless.

"What do you expect me to say to that? What do you want me to do?"

She shrugged. "Tell me I'm not making a total ass of myself. Forgive me?"

Forgive her?

He faced the road, staring out into the lush landscape, letting the tropical breeze cool his anger and his ardor. He shifted slowly into first. His healing had already begun. Last night had proved it.

He wanted her.

"I'm working on it," he said.

He suspected that she was disappointed in his answer. But Diane had taught him well, all those years ago, to be cautious. He wasn't willing to give in at her bidding.

He demonstrated the function of the three floor pedals, and how two were used when shifting gears. Diane was a good student, as he knew she would be, if for no other reason than she hated to fail. She caught on quickly to the mechanics. After only a half dozen attempts that stalled, she finally nailed it, finding her own touch and feel of the shift stick.

Hale became the passenger as she drove through different streets and situations in and around the always crowded center of Cruz Bay. After an hour, he suggested they stop for a break and they sat outside a food truck that served only conch fritters. They shared a plate, along with cold beers and pleasant conversation. They stayed away from any mention of the kiss they had shared or their feelings about it. He wondered if Diane was frustrated. Hale wondered if she was aware that so was he.

Afterward Diane took over the driving again, getting ever-more adventurous on the steep and narrow roads of the island. Near the top of a rise as she attempted to shift for the down run, the car stalled. It nearly caused an accident with another car fast approaching from behind. The second car screeched to a stop when Hale and Diane rolled back several feet. Hale felt his whole body brace for impact and he was about to reach over to shift for her when Diane, gritting her teeth with determination, muttered to him, "Don't even think about it."

She shifted roughly. They jerked forward several times and then got going.

Hale couldn't help laughing when they were clear of the hill.

"Damn! You haven't changed a bit."

She didn't answer for a moment and then said, rather reflectively, "Only where it matters."

He thought about that. He hoped so, too.

Hale instructed her to drive to a location she wasn't familiar with, inland. Then, he showed her the GPS system, and how to enter a starting point and a destination that the system could then map.

"I want you to take us back to the post office," Hale said to her. "We can pick up Simon from the dock afterward."

He had her enter the address for the location from a service directory for Cruz Bay that was in the glove compartment. The system came on and began to talk in a digital female voice directing her where to drive, how far, when to turn and even when to slow down to stay within the speed limits. Hale was glad to see that she was like a kid with a new toy. She said she loved that it did most of the work for her.

"I think I'm going to buy stock in this company," she announced triumphantly when she'd pulled into a parking spot opposite the post office entrance.

They left the car there and walked to the dock to wait for the ferry from Red Hook. Again, the pier was busy with people waiting for arriving passengers, and those waiting to board for the return to St. Thomas. And with nothing to do but wait, he could tell that they were both, again, remembering the flirtation between them that seemed to be escalating.

He was staring off into the distance, idly watching the approach of the ferry. He realized Diane was staring at him and he shifted his gaze. She slowly, silently, smiled at him. He began to get aroused.

Hale didn't want his private parts to do his thinking for him.

He remembered how stunning she looked in her formal attire the night of the gala in Baltimore. She'd fulfilled the promise she'd shown as a seventeen-year-old and then some. She was tall and slender, graceful in a totally unselfconscious way. What had once been budding breasts, small but firm, had reached their maturity and were fuller. She moved her body, sitting and standing, like a woman who'd had experience with the opposite sex and was confident of her attraction. He looked away briefly, drawing in a deep breath. Hale wondered what part he'd played in that.

She stood close to him. Casually, as if she had no choice because of all the people. Occasionally, she brushed against him. But somehow he knew that

THE EDITOR'S "THANK YOU" FREE GIFTS INCLUDE:

➤ Two Kimani™ Romance Novels
➤ Two exciting surprise gifts

YES! I have placed my Editor's "thank you" Free Gifts seal in the space provided at right. Please send me 2 FREE books, and my 2 FREE Mystery Gifts. I understand that I am under no obligation to purchase anything further, as explained on the back of this card.

PLACE
FREE GIFTS
SEAL
HERE

About how many NEW paperback fiction books have you purchased in the past 3 months?

❑ 0-2   ❑ 3-6   ❑ 7 or more

E7XY   E5MH   E5MT

168/368 XDL

Please Print

FIRST NAME

LAST NAME

ADDRESS

APT.#   CITY

STATE/PROV.   ZIP/POSTAL CODE

Thank You!

BUSINESS REPLY MAIL

FIRST-CLASS MAIL   PERMIT NO. 717   BUFFALO, NY

POSTAGE WILL BE PAID BY ADDRESSEE

THE READER SERVICE
PO BOX 1867
BUFFALO NY 14240-9952

NO POSTAGE
NECESSARY
IF MAILED
IN THE
UNITED STATES

every move, every gesture, was calculated and with a purpose.

A little annoyed by Diane's tactic, Hale nonetheless realized it was working.

The ferry came in and followed the usual routine of disgorging its passengers and freight. He'd never met Simon, Diane's other half-brother. But the instant he came off the gangplank Hale knew who he was. He'd learned that Diane's mother had married a white man, and their son was fair skinned, tall and athletic. He had the kind of good looks that caused second glances and long stares. Hale could see that Simon knew his own appeal, but didn't need to play on it. In that, he was much like his older sister.

He strolled down the pier toward them with confidence and ease. He had an expensive-looking heavy leather duffel bag, a leather jacket stuck through the handles he held and a computer case hanging from his shoulder. He was dressed in casual black chinos and a beige cashmere sweater with the sleeves pushed up to his elbows. Dark glasses hid his gaze, which served to emphasis his square jaw and wide full mouth that was breaking into a slow broad smile...with perfect teeth.

"There he is," Diane announced, unnecessarily, and started toward him.

Hale stayed back to witness the greeting between brother and sister. It was amusing to witness, as well, the way people around them stood back and deferred, not sure who he was but acting as if a celebrity that they couldn't quite place had just arrived in their midst.

Diane and Simon embraced, and it was clear that the love between them was fast and genuine. Again Hale was reminded of his lack of family and what he did not have. The Maxwells' generous love aside, he was still sorry for the loss of his parents and his brother.

Introductions were made for his sake. He and Simon, to his surprise, exchanged a fist pound. He waited until they were in the Jeep before announcing that he wasn't returning to the house with them. Hale deliberately avoided Diane's puzzled and, if he was correct, displeased gaze. That didn't make him change his mind. More than ever he felt the need to put a little distance between himself and the extended Maxwell clan.

He asked to be dropped off on a service road that would allow him to walk the distance back to the bay where the *Paradise* Zodiac was moored.

"You did good today," Hale whispered quickly to Diane as he climbed out of the Jeep and let Simon take his seat.

"Keep an eye on her," he said, only half joking, to Simon. "She only graduated to standard in the last few hours."

Her look of utter disappointment got to him. He winked at her as she pulled away.

Diane returned to the living room from the kitchen, where she'd unloaded the dishwasher and put everything away from dinner. It had given her some time alone to think about what was happening to her feelings about Hale.

In the living room she walked into a high-energy, laughter-filled conversation with anecdotes from Simon, which had made him the center of attention all evening. She wasn't surprised. She'd known, even as a little girl, when her mother and stepfather had him, that it was impossible to dislike, resent or feel any jealousy toward her younger brother. He had always been the most even-tempered person she'd ever known. Even as he grew into full awareness of his attraction and his effect on people...particularly females...she'd never known Simon to use that to his advantage. He never needed to.

This was the first time, ever, that he was meeting her father and Eva, the kids and Hale. And he'd become very much at home among them all in no time flat.

Her anxiety over how Simon would behave, and how he would be received, turned out to be for nothing. She could relax once she'd taken him to check into his guesthouse for the three days he was going to be on the island and had driven him up to the house in Chocolate Hole for dinner and the evening with everyone.

She wondered why Hale had chosen not to spend the evening with them. With *her*. She missed him.

Diane knew when a man was attracted to her. The way they'd kissed, with complete abandon and hunger. The way she'd instantly begun to get moist and pool between her legs, wanting to press against him to increase the feelings or release the already built-up tension.

She moved from one chair to another. Crossed her legs, squeezed her thighs.

Mistake.

She uncrossed them. She looked at the time. After nine.

The novelty of a new person in the house wore off and the kids went down to the converted garage where there was a flat-screen TV. The sounds of screeching car brakes, explosions and gunfire wafted up from below.

Finally, Simon stretched and declared he should be getting back to his hotel. He thanked Adam and Eva for inviting him to join them on St. John.

"I can drive you back," Adam volunteered at once.

"No, I'll take him," Diane said smoothly. "I need to pick up a few things at the convenience store."

Not giving her father a chance to object, she went into her room to get her things, pausing to get a heavier sweater and stuffing it into her tote. She stood waiting by the rented Jeep as Simon bid good-night to everyone.

"We're not going to wait up for you," Adam said, waving from the veranda.

Now she had no trouble driving the standard vehicle, but she went slowly because it was dark. There was still a lot of life around Mongoose Junction and Cruz Bay as Diane drove through the town to the small guesthouse overlooking Frank Bay. Diane promised that she'd pick him up the next day for breakfast and a tour of the island. They said good-night and he walked to his condo unit.

Diane made her stop at the late-night convenience store and left town again. She drove to the marina in the bay where the *Paradise* was anchored, pulling off the road under a tree.

She stripped down to her swimsuit and put a few items into a plastic bag. She forced as much of the air out as she could before closing it and then used an inexpensive belt to secure it to her waist. With a sure memory of the beach and the drop-off about ten feet out into the water, she began to breaststroke out to the sloop.

She thought nothing of the steps being down and climbed aboard, stepping cautiously on the deck. It was quiet, although there were lights on below. There was a pair of large male sandals near the steps leading below. But no sign of Hale.

Diane realized that she was breathing hard. Not in exertion from the swim but in anticipation. She released the belt around her waist and it dropped to the deck with the plastic bag. She swept her wet hair back from her face, looking quickly around.

"Hale?"

There was no response.

She went a few steps down into the hole and called again, although it was obvious he wasn't below either. Puzzled, Diane began walking toward the bow of the sloop to see if perhaps he was sleeping under the stars on several of the air cushions. She had just reached the position of the headsail when she heard the sounds behind her. Someone was climbing up the aft stairs from the water onto the ship.

A head appeared dripping water, and then a broad bare torso, glistening wet, as strong arms hoisted Hale up. And then the rest of him appeared.

Hale stepped onto the deck frowning, his eyes following the wet footprints she'd left. Diane stared, riveted in place, her breath catching in her throat as their gazes met.

He was stark naked, water dripping from every part of him.

Chapter 7

She didn't try *not* to let her gaze drop to Hale's exposed attributes, the mere sight of which began a chain reaction of sensations within her.

Like him, she was also wet from her swim. Although the tepid breeze cooled her skin, Diane felt a flush of heat beneath, a tingling on her nerve ends.

"Was that your idea of a cold shower?" she asked, her voice quiet and suggestive.

His shock at seeing her turned into a scowl and he started a slow walk toward her. He made no attempt to cover himself.

Her mouth felt suddenly dry.

"How did you get here?"

Her chin went up, challenging his annoyance.

"I drove. Then I swam."

"You know better than to do that alone. Adam..."

"Are you going to tell on me?" she boldly teased.

Hale stopped two feet from her, suddenly appearing so much taller than she could recall. So indomitable. Unbelievably sexy.

"What are you doing here?"

His tone had changed. Questioning and skeptical.

She swallowed and took a chance.

"Don't you know? I'm not deaf, dumb or blind, Hale. My sensory perceptions are pretty sharp. I bet yours are, too. We've been honing in on each other."

He narrowed his gaze, not giving an inch.

"So?"

If anything Diane knew she'd made the right decision in taking matters into her own hands. She knew that if she waited on Hale, it would be a snowy day in hell before he made the first move. She understood why, but she didn't want to wait that long. Something had to be done while she felt so hot. So that she could sleep at night.

"So…I think we should do something about it. Don't you?"

She took a step closer to him, letting her gaze drift across his torso, at his firm pecs and hard male nipples and the tight sprinkle of dark hair. She boldly let her attention drop once more to find that he was no longer limp or curved to the ground, but was on a slow and steady rise. Getting hard. The base was embedded in a dark forest of curly hair with a thin trail growing toward his navel. She clinched her pelvic muscles, trying to control the fluttering down there. When the time came she wanted those hot contractions she'd been feeling to be around something. Him.

"I'm not eighteen anymore, Diane. I don't play games. And I don't have anything to prove."

Diane brought her gaze, bright and expectant, up to

his, and had the satisfaction of seeing that his eyes were also filled with desire. Or lust. He couldn't disguise it.

"I came because I knew I had to. Maybe I'm taking a risk, Hale. But do you really want me to leave? While you're like…*that?*"

The scowl turned to a thoughtful frown.

"I don't know yet if I can trust you."

"Give me a chance to change your mind."

She reached behind her back and pulled the tie of her bikini top and the one around her neck. Never taking her gaze from his, Diane took the piece and dropped it on the deck. Hale's eyes clouded over.

"You told me last night I don't really need it."

"That was last…" That's as far as he managed.

Diane felt the tip of his penis extend and brush against her groin.

"I've been having this dream. About that time we were together," she said, her voice a breathy whisper. "About…what you did to me that night."

"That's what you wanted. I scared you."

"I hated you for it. Because…I…liked it. You made me feel ashamed that I liked it."

His jaw tightened and clenched. "Now you tell me?"

"I want you to do it again."

Diane stepped even closer until her breasts pressed gently against him. Hale tentatively slid his arms around her, pulling her closer still until they touched chest to knees, his thickening penis almost tucked between her thighs. His hands cupped around her buttocks. With a deep inhalation as his eyes drifted close, he ground her hips against him.

Diane's mouth opened and she uttered a weak moan.

She put her arms around his neck, lifting her lips blindly to find his kiss.

It was just what she needed then, hot and deep and all consuming. Their lips worked together with a deliberate slowness that left her dizzy and disoriented. Their hips together, the full pleasure of joining thwarted by her bikini briefs. Together their breathing melded and hissed like a whisper in their ears with a growing urgency. The prelude was rich with promise and they took their time to enjoy each movement and touch. The intensity was building up until they both felt it in the rush of blood through their veins, the throbbing in their groins that edged toward release.

Suddenly Diane pulled her mouth free, momentarily teasing him with her lips, the tip of her tongue. Her breasts points were so tender and sensitive they ached.

"Do it again," she pleaded.

With obvious difficulty and reluctance, Hale took several unsteady steps back, releasing her. As if suddenly remembering that they stood on the open deck of a sailboat that was anchored within shouting distance of other crafts, he glanced quickly around and then back to her, his eyes now filled with purpose.

"Go up front."

As she did so, she could hear his movements behind her. It went nighttime dark when he turned out the lights below deck. She waited, seated on the raised forecastle of the deck. He returned slowly, carrying something. It turned out to be two small cushions and a lightweight quilt that, together, they spread over the surface. Once done, Diane stretched out on her back, staring at the magnificent beauty of the night, but for the moment unable to concentrate or appreciate the sight. She waited.

He loomed over her, staring down. She seductively threw her arms back over her head and arched her back. Her breasts jutted out. Offering herself up to him. And wanting him to take her.

"Hale," she said simply in invitation.

He bent over her, crouched between her raised knees to cup her breasts, knead them, kiss and lick the tips, while she undulated and quietly panted. He stayed with it until her nipples were hard extended buttons. Hale let go of her breasts with a tender kiss on each one. He slid his hands down her torso to her stomach, causing the muscles to contract. His lips and kisses followed in their wake. His fingers caught under the top of her briefs and peeled them down her legs, dropping them to the deck.

Suddenly, he disappeared, kneeling between her legs, out of sight.

She felt him began to nuzzle through the soft hair between her legs. Diane held her breath. She stiffened her body, drew in her stomach...waiting. Then, she felt the warmth of his breath, his lips and tongue.

She let her body relax, her breath out with a long moan, and she let the most exquisite sensations assail her that she'd ever known. He was totally and freely willing to go *there*. Her mind and body centered and focused as she put her entire being into what Hale was doing to her with the tip of his tongue, the sucking of his mouth. She could barely breathe because of the delicious feelings he was creating. She squeezed her eyes closed, her breathing now labored as the delicate stroking of his tongue brought her to the edge of oblivion. She reached out to grip his shoulders, her fingers digging into the firm cool flesh. She held on as he encouraged her, stimulated her, pushed her irrevocably over the precipice.

She rode the cresting wave of pleasure, not caring if it might kill her. She moaned deeply with each drawn-out breath as she came.

Afterward, all she could do was lie there, exposed and satiated and vulnerable and as if every bone in her body had gone soft.

She had been waiting for this feeling since she was seventeen. She'd wanted Hale alone to give it to her.

Diane could do nothing, for the moment, to help Hale. To reach out to him and give at least as good as she'd gotten. She couldn't move.

She felt his body next to hers. He stretched on his side and eased himself close, turning her into his arms. He flipped a corner of the quilt to partially cover their bare bodies against the Caribbean air. Diane curled against him, feeling a contentment that took her by surprise.

He was so quiet that she, on the verge of dozing off, wondered if he had. She snuggled closer. He smoothed his large hand slowly up and down her back, erotically teasing his fingertips along a thigh and over her butt.

"Is that what you wanted?" he asked very quietly, his voice gravely and deep.

"Yes."

"Is that all?"

Is that all?

It was an unexpected question and she didn't know the answer. For now she was happy to be held by him, with care and tenderness and...

"No," Diane admitted.

He sighed deeply. "I don't understand Di. Why now?"

Di!

When they were teenagers he used to call her Princess Di because, he'd said at the time, she acted like she was so special everyone should do exactly what she wanted. But Hale had been the only one who never would.

"I misjudged you. I seem to do that a lot with people."

"Your ex?"

She hid her face against his chest. Nodded silently.

"I finally figured out why you did it to me that way the first time. You thought I was a virgin. You were trying to protect me."

"Yeah. I was."

"And I thought…"

"You thought it was some low-class act that nice girls like you didn't do. Back then, none of your sorry ass boyfriends would think to try and make it good for you."

Hale had. Then and now.

She had to smile to herself at that. She'd lost her virginity just the semester before, while on a school exchange program in Munich, Germany. The boy had been from Italy, a fellow classmate. Gorgeous and bold, he had been relentless, charming and funny in his pursuit of her. And he'd been experienced. But still, the first time was difficult. It certainly got better. But she'd not been transported, or felt any of the touted euphoria seen in movies and read in books.

Until that night with Hale when she'd teased and challenged him. And he'd taken her up on it.

Diane snuggled closer to him, entwining their legs, playing footsie.

"I guess you want a full disclosure about why I was so nasty to you."

His hand glided back and forth across her stomach.

His fingertips lightly drifted through her pubic hair. Close enough for Diane to want him to explore further.

"I just gave you the thrill of a lifetime. I think you owe me a lot more than apologies. But go for it. I'm listening."

For a moment all Diane could think of was all those years when Hale was under her father's tutelage, denying herself...them...the chance to develop an honest passion for each other.

Maybe.

Diane twisted her head to kiss the arm that cradled her head.

"We weren't from the same kind of background."

"I got that part," Hale drawled. "You used to piss me off with your attitude."

"And I thought you didn't care what I thought of you. And then there was another thing that was happening to me. You made me hot."

"Excuse me?"

"You know what I mean," she murmured. "On the one hand, I wanted to hate you. On the other, I was so attracted to you. I used to have the most...incredible fantasies about you. The two of us, together."

He said nothing for a few seconds and then Hale began to laugh softly.

"I didn't think it was so funny," she complained.

"You could have had me if you'd acted right. I would have scratched your itch. You could have done the same for me."

"Well, we did..."

"Yeah, the night Adam and Eva went out. Suddenly you're all over me."

"I had nothing to lose, but you didn't know that. My

virginity was not the issue. I was having wet dreams about you."

Hale grunted, his hand pushing further between her legs. "Testing me, huh?"

"Something like that." She sighed, shifting her legs to give him room.

"Well?"

"I wasn't disappointed. You went far…"

"And *below*…"

"The call of duty."

"Glad I finally got your attention…"

He wasn't angry about it, and it was a revelation that they could even talk about it now, openly, without ill feelings but real surprise. At least, on her part.

Diane wondered if she hadn't acted so imperial with Hale back then and pulled her Princess Di act, if she'd given him half a chance, how different their relationship might have been.

Or not.

Then came the inevitable comparison with her ex-husband Trevor.

She cringed. Not a good idea. Trevor was everything that Hale was not. But the reverse was also true. Trevor had been the acceptable black man model. He was from the right kind of family and attended the right schools. He had the right social contacts and was one of the few successful black financial brokers in D.C. He had manners and standards, and would have been put off by even the idea of doing what Hale had done for her. *Twice.*

She now realized and accepted that the failure of their two-year marriage was her fault. Her expectations had never been on the same page with her desires. Not having them met by Trevor had forced her into work and more work for solace…leaving him behind. She had been stunned when Trevor had walked out. His action had embarrassed her.

Diane suddenly shivered as another thought exploded into her awareness. If she'd been honest as a young woman she might have recognized that it was not someone like Trevor she wanted. But someone who shaped up to be more like Hale…and the man he'd become.

She absently let her hand glide up and down his torso. His skin was warm and she was absorbing his body heat. Her fingers teased at one of his nipples and then played in the hollow of his navel. He shifted slightly under her hand, and she felt his erect penis touch her hand.

Diane let her hand stroke him slowly, tickling and titillating the shaft, down through the hair. He lay and let her explore, his body responding to her every move. She heard a faint grunt.

"Are you going to do something about this or just torture me?" he murmured, his voice strained.

Diane came up on her elbow and tried to look into his face. Her hand continued stimulating him. His hips beginning to undulate at her touch.

"I think we've put it off long enough, don't you?"

With her words he placed his hand behind her head and brought it down so they could kiss. The meeting of their lips and tongues immediately brought her to a state of arousal. Hale moved, forcing her to release him, and he put her on her back, all the while kissing her until she felt that lazy drifting of her mind and the taking over of her senses.

Suddenly he dragged his mouth free, muttering an oath of frustration.

"Listen…sorry about this. I'm not prepared…"

"I am," she managed. "On the deck. The bag…the plastic bag…"

Hale lifted himself away, and a wave of night air washed over her skin.

Hurry, she said to herself. *Hurry…*

"Got it," Hale said, rummaging through the contents of the bag. Soon he was returning to her.

Diane reached up her arms to him, welcoming him. They began to kiss again and Hale settled between her legs as her knees fell open. They were panting, but almost as if by mutual consent they didn't want to rush. Hale's urgency quickly became apparent. He'd been waiting longer than she had for satisfaction.

He came forward with his hips and unerringly lodged himself, smoothly sliding deep to complete their connection.

They moved together, perfectly matched and fitted, their bodies in rhythm as they strived for release from their raging delirium. Diane clung to him, her mouth searching for him. The intensity of her kiss and his sensitivity finally reached the tipping point.

Hale uttered something primal and guttural as he pulsed and climaxed within her. The rocking of his hips set off the fireworks within her and she peaked again.

She lay beneath him, enjoying his weight and warmth, feeling protected. The irony of the two of them together like this did not escape her. Diane thought of how her father and Eva had honored her wishes to not talk about Hale, and so she had missed not only his coming of age, his maturity, but him. By insisting that they not share any of her life with him, he'd not seen nor experienced that she'd tried very hard to overcome his scathing indictment of her as a self-centered "Princess," not for his sake but her own.

She hugged him and kissed the side of his neck. She felt the still-rapid pulsing of a vein.

"Can you imagine if we'd waited any longer?" she conjectured, her tone languid and drowsy, and amazed.

"Shoot me now," Hale muttered against her shoulder. He grew flaccid and slipped out. "Consider that rain check paid in full."

They stood on the veranda and waved as the Jeep reversed in the small parking area and then headed down the driveway.

"We'll see you in a little while," Diane shouted.

"Not me," Adam added.

Diane and Eva laughed, as her father had made it perfectly clear that he was just about holiday-companied out. He intended to do nothing for the rest of the day but watch some TV and sleep.

Hayden had already been picked up by a local friend who was going out fishing with his father and brother. Hale had already called to say he was hanging out on the sloop for most of the day. He'd brought down work to do. He was working on an important brief for a hearing coming up early in the new year. It seemed to Diane that there was not going to be an opportunity for them to be together today and she was disappointed.

Unlike the day before, Diane reminisced, when just the two of them had taken the Zodiac and skiffed over to a small cay between Trunk and Cinnamon Bay to swim and picnic. Hayden and Adam had gone to pick up supplies from a boat shop in Coral Bay. Eva had settled on the veranda with a book, and the girls had slept late, limiting their options to join any of them, for which Diane had been grateful. Simon had decided to hang around Cruz Bay, have breakfast and explore the small town.

The beach she and Hale ended up on was small... and deserted. They'd anchored in the shallow surf and explored the secluded area for other accesses to the beach. There were none. Diane had been thrilled that she and Hale had it all to themselves.

"I think my father used to come here to collect samples," she told Hale as she stripped off her cover-up. "Eva said he taught her to snorkel here, and she didn't even know how to swim."

Hale had come up behind her, his strong arms circling her waist and pulling her back against his chest. He kissed the back of her neck.

"While we're here I have something else in mind."

She turned in his arms to look into his face. She decided he had the most beautiful mouth. She ran a thumb over the surface of his lips as he stared at her, his gaze hooded and filled with warmth. She could already feel herself getting moist, wet, in that place where he'd so effectively used his mouth and tongue on her the night before, under the stars. The look in his eyes had completely changed in less than twenty-four hours. That wary look of suspicion and distance was, magically, gone.

She'd kissed him briefly and pulled away.

"You'll have to wait. I want to swim first."

They'd frolicked and swam in the aquamarine water until they were tired and hungry. Under the low-hanging canopy of a sea grape tree they'd had a lunch of Eva's homemade chicken salad, raisin pecan rolls, brownies and strawberry iced tea. Full and warm and sleepy, they'd spread out the towels in the shade. Assured that they were alone, they relieved each other of bothersome swimsuits and made slow, sensual, heated love until their bodies were sleek with sweat and further satiated with pleasure.

They'd drifted off to sleep spooned together, risking discovery, and awakened almost an hour later to drowsy arousal. After making love again they'd cooled off in the bay before putting their suits back on and heading back to Chocolate Hole.

But that night had not given them an opportunity to repeat their adventure of the night before. Still, Diane had had one of the most restful sleeps she'd experienced in months, with dreams that were fanciful and romantic....

The memory made Diane smile secretly. It would have to sustain her for the day, not knowing for sure when they could be together again. She was already preparing excuses for slipping away later.

She didn't hear a word Eva was saying as they headed back into the house. Adam had already disappeared to entertain himself.

"...sure if he believed me," Eva murmured, going to get her purse from the sofa.

"What?" Diane asked, doing the same.

"I said, your father didn't understand why you and I didn't go with the girls and Simon. He wanted to know why we're meeting them later."

"What did you tell him?" Diane asked, frowning. She understood Eva's desire that Adam not know of her medical concerns.

"I had to lie, of course, and I feel terrible about that. I didn't tell him you thought I should have a sonogram. I told him you wanted to see the cardiac department at the hospital. That you were curious what the facility preparations were in case of a serious emergency."

Diane cringed. "That's a little close for comfort," she said.

"I thought it was better to stay close to the truth. That way I won't forget what I said in case he starts asking questions later."

"Well, the possibility of fibroids is all I think we're looking at. But I understand how you feel."

After the visit to the hospital Diane drove them into Cruz Bay to meet up with Bailey and Courtney for lunch and shopping.

It was Eva who ended the excursion into Cruz Bay with the simple announcement that she was ready to go back to the house. The girls, worn out from the crowds and walking, did not put up a fuss. Diane offered to drive them back, knowing without being told that her brother was already planning his evening. But he surprised her when he suggested she return in the evening, maybe with Hale, and they'd have dinner together. Somewhere they could listen to music.

Diane was the last one to enter the house behind the girls, who'd stampeded up the stairs, and Eva, who had immediately gone in search of her husband. Eva found him stretched out on the sofa, reading *Time*. Diane pretended not to witness their loving greeting, warm and palpable after mere hours apart.

That's what I want, she said plaintively to herself. And she had an image of being on the beach with Hale. Of having him awaken her with a sleepy kiss before they'd made love again. There had been this feeling inside of her, this…euphoria, because he was being so loving and gentle.

That's what I want.

Chapter 8

The rain added an unexpected calm to the evening. Unintentionally, it also put the holiday into perspective, as well. All the exuberant partying that had been going on for a week on the island was winding down. The seemingly endless days of sunshine and blue skies and tranquil seas were also at an end. At least for the evening. Everyone was anticipating New Year's Eve to be perfect. The year was going to end on a warm tropic breeze.

But tonight was a date night, suggested by Simon. It felt good to Diane to be just with people her own age. It was wonderful to be having a real date with Hale.

Diane sipped her wine, sitting back in the wicker lounge chair at the pool bar of the Westin Hotel with her legs crossed. Hale was next to her, cool and handsome in startling white linen slacks and a black short-sleeved loose shirt tucked into the waist. He was addressing

remarks to Katie, a pretty black woman who managed
a gallery near the pier, and whom Simon had met and
invited to join them just hours earlier. Katie was wearing
a gauzy black sundress with an elastic waistline that
emphasized her tiny middle. Her medium-length hair
had been two-strand twisted and then released, giving
her a bushy do of corkscrew curls that complimented
her heart-shaped face. Diane listened and watched her
brother in action with his date, at his charming best.

How does he do it? she wondered, amused.

She liked Katie. She left Houston after a nasty divorce
and escaped to lick her wounds with an aunt and uncle
who lived on St. Thomas. That had been three years ago
and she was not yet ready to return to the mainland.

"I guess I'm the only one here who's never been
married and divorced," Simon commented, ordering
another round of drinks.

Diane's attention swiveled quickly to Hale. She raised
her brows at him as if to say, "excuse me?"

He held her gaze, composed and easy. "I don't think
I'd count being divorced as a badge of honor exactly. It's
painful and it's hard. It's a part of my experience that I
failed at."

She said nothing, realizing she could hardly call Hale
on the fact that she had no idea he'd been married. He
had known about Trevor.

What else didn't she know about him?

"I'm too young," Simon said blithely, causing
everyone to laugh.

"I agree," Diane added, hiding her surprise at the
revelation about Hale but merely smiling at him.
Beneath the marble cocktail table between their chairs
he reached for her hand to hold. She welcomed it but
her curiosity did not abate.

"Simon tells me you're a doctor," Katie said to her. "That's great. My dad's an internist. They used to call them family doctors."

"Everyone specializes now."

"He's always complaining about the HMOs and the pharmaceuticals. There's so much pressure to do things a certain way if you want to make a decent living."

Diane looked at her. "What things?"

Katie made a vague gesture with her hand. "Oh, I'm sure you know. The sample drugs to give to patients. The extra tests. And then there's the kickbacks from the drug companies to prescribe their brands. One of my father's colleagues had his license revoked for doing that. He can't practice for five years."

Everyone grew quiet, not sure what to say about the dark side of the medical business.

"Our station did a three-part special on the problem about two years ago," Simon commented. "It's pretty widespread."

"There's a lot of money involved," Hale added. "I know. I used to work for Carlyle when I finished law school."

"You did?" Diane found herself asking.

"Yeah, my father talked about Carlyle. Not an honest company."

Hale chortled. "No, they weren't. But for a while they were pulling in serious bucks."

The conversation got swept away quickly from the subject of drug companies to Katie's anecdotes about some of her father's patients.

But Diane only half listened, still caught up on Hale's confession that he'd worked for a company that had had repeated criminal charges filed against them. All she could think of was those pills that Eva had been taking that another company had produced and tried to pawn off on unsuspecting and trusting consumers.

He didn't seem embarrassed to admit he'd worked for such a place. Now she *really* wondered what else about Hale's background he had not told her. Her father always insisted that Hale had turned his life around, had seriously changed from the young teen he'd been when Adam had first met him. But it was also said that the fruit doesn't fall far from the tree.

The rain not only continued, it became heavy, pelting the walking paths and the roof of the overhang where they sat, protected. It created a shimmering gray curtain that cooled the air and, one by one, the couples around them finished and left.

"I think I'd better get Katie back or we'll end up having to swim," Simon said, now signaling for the check.

But Hale beat him to it, settling the tab and thanking Simon for suggesting the evening.

"I was going to take Di out anyway, but this was great. A really nice evening. Good to meet you Katie," Hale said with a smile for the other woman.

"Hearing all of you talk about your lives back in the States…well, it made me think for the first time, maybe I should get back to the real world and a real life," Katie said wryly.

"I don't know." Simon shook his head as they slowly headed to the exit of the hotel and the parking lot. "Life seems pretty laid-back down here. I could do this for a while."

"And what will you tell Mom about dropping out and becoming a beach bum? I don't think so," Diane said caustically. Everyone laughed.

They stood around the open entrance, adjacent to

the front desk of the hotel, and continued to chat in a hope that the rain would ease up. It did not. Finally, they decided to say good-night and be on their way. Simon and Katie left first, making a mad dash to Simon's rented Jeep. They didn't have far to go, since Katie was renting a small cottage just off of Great Cruz Bay.

By the time Diane and Hale had gotten into his Jeep, wet and breathless from running, the rain seemed to have taken on the personality of an angry, torrential summer storm. They'd only gone a mile from the hotel on the approach to the marina and the road to Chocolate Hole when they were stopped by a roadblock of local police cars, their lights flashing, and several emergency and fire vehicles.

A water tanker had run off the road on a steep and curving turn, totally blocking traffic in both directions. The driver had been hurt and had been loaded into an ambulance that was still parked behind the accident. It was going to be some time before the truck could be moved. The heavy rain was not going to make it easier.

Diane and Hale sat for a minute, discussing their options, but it was Hale who made the decision. He used his cell phone and dialed the house. Hayden answered and at Hale's request put Adam on the line.

"There's an accident just outside of Cruz Bay. We can't use the road back to the house. It makes sense for Diane to stay down here tonight."

He glanced at her, not for consent but to make sure she understood. She silently nodded, the implications bouncing like sunbeams around her mind.

"Yeah, we'll be careful. I'll drive her back up in the morning, assuming the road's open."

When the call ended, Hale turned in his seat to face

her, his hand on her shoulder while his fingers gently massaged her smooth skin. His gaze held hers.

"Look, I think we can cut around this and make it back to the marina. We can take the Zodiac to the *Paradise* and stay there for the night. We're going to get very wet and it's going to be a bit cramped."

"Or?" she asked when he hesitated.

"We can see if there's a room at the hotel."

Diane blinked at him. The very first thought that came to her mind was that there'd be a real bed. A *big* bed. And they'd be able to share it for the whole night. There'd be a shower and a terrace...and room service. And comfortable privacy.

"Let's go back to the hotel," she said.

He broke into a slow, wide grin. Straightening in his seat, Hale carefully turned around to head back into town. There was enough traffic to make progress slow. What should have taken five minutes took nearly thirty. And, to their relief, there were a few rooms available.

The room was on the third floor, overlooking Pillsbury Sound and St. Thomas in the background. But because of the rain there wasn't much to see. They silently explored the nicely appointed room with its queen bed, love seat sofa, cool, tiled floor and ceiling fan.

Alone in the room, it was the first time Diane had a true realization that they had become lovers. That they had begun an exploration of each other. But she was also aware, suddenly, that their knowledge was pretty much of a physical nature. She'd learned a lot about Hale since the holidays began, but it seemed he'd always known quite a bit more about her.

She walked toward him because he was waiting and she needed to have his arms around her. She needed the reassurance that this was not a passing fancy or a mere tryst for either of them.

The question was, where did she want it to go?

Hale enveloped her in his arms, squeezing her against him as he kissed her forehead, her cheek, and searched for her mouth. She made it easy for him. She so liked kissing Hale; it felt like he wanted to please her, make her feel good.

Nonetheless she now recognized that what she didn't know about him could hurt her. That didn't stop her.

Diane kissed him back and it was as tender as it was arousing. He played with her lips and then released them.

"How about some wine? I feel like celebrating."

She leaned back within the circle of his arms, their hips pressed together. She cupped his face with her hands. It was so strong and masculine. His eyes so... intense.

"What are we celebrating?"

"You staying with me for the whole night. No midnight run back to the house on the hill." She laughed lightly with him. "I was beginning to feel like a teenager again, sneaking around behind your parents' back. Waiting to get caught and trying to explain..."

She frowned at him when he stopped. "Explain what?"

Hale seemed to ponder her question and his answer. He finally shook his head slightly. "That I care too much about you, and them, to ever do anything to hurt you."

He stepped out of their embrace and went to the phone. He called to request a bottle of Shiraz and two glasses.

While he did so Diane wandered out to the terrace, closing the sliding door behind her. She needed a moment to think about what was happening. Taking her teenage dream the full distance had been exciting and gratifying in the extreme. Far better than the dream, actually. She loved being with Hale. She loved making love with him. She no longer even pretended not to, although it was a little galling to have to concede her liking to her father and Eva. But so what? The fact remained, he wasn't the least bit like she'd thought he'd be. Hale had grown up to be so much more of a man than she had imagined. And yet...

And yet...

The door slid open and closed behind her. She felt his presence without turning around. Then, his arms slipped around her waist as he stood behind her. Diane crossed her arms over her chest, extended her hands so that she could touch him. She let her head rest against his chest, let her eyes drift close.

He did everything right.

And yet...

"Doesn't look like it's going to let up, does it?" he said in a deep, reflective voice.

Her mind focused, came back to where they stood, with the rain pouring down beyond their haven. "Maybe it won't. Maybe it will rain for forty days and forty nights."

"Shame. Then we're stuck here in this room together."

"Are you complaining?"

He squeezed her. "Does it sound or feel like a complaint?"

"We could be trapped on the sloop, you know."

Hale groaned, burying his mouth in her hair. "It's going to be so nice to make love on a bed that doesn't rock."

She turned around, gazing into his eyes, pressing and rotating her hips and pleased by Hale's immediate response. "Or a room that doesn't sway."

"And to wake up in each other's arms."

She caught her breath. That did sound...*very* nice.

"I didn't know you were married," she said flatly.

Her statement clearly caught him off guard. Hale sighed and frowned at her.

"We were in law school together. Her background was not much different from mine. We both were lucky to get the chance to do better. We bonded. We were going to change the system. Do more for poor people. We fell in love. Bad reasons to fall in love.

"She had a temper and she didn't like to compromise. Her street creds kept getting in the way of her work and our marriage. I wanted to move beyond all that. She didn't know how."

"That why you divorced?"

He nodded. "That and other things. She told me I'd sold out. I said being a professional victim doesn't play anymore. Adam taught me that."

Diane was surprised how moved she was by his story. Not that Hale's marriage didn't work out, but she totally related to how emotionally wrenching it was to be so wrong. It seemed that everyone she knew had had a starter marriage. Not exactly something to be proud of, just a fact of life. It was just hard to get it right the first time.

"Hale, I didn't know..."

He kissed her hard to make her shut up.

"There's a lot about me you don't know. Don't try to figure it all out tonight, okay?"

Hale turned and went back into the bedroom. Diane followed, watching him. He didn't seem angry so much as tired. She wanted to know about Carlyle, but he was right. Playing twenty questions was not the way to do it. Nor was it the best use of the time they had together.

Diane went up behind him and circled him around the waist. She laid her cheek against his back. He was tense, but he covered her hands with his to hold them in place.

"I hate that we have to go back day after tomorrow."

"Me, too," he murmured. "It's been a great holiday, Di. Because of you. And us."

She nodded. "I think so."

Hale pulled her around to stand in front of him. "Out with the old?"

She smiled at him softly. "In with the new."

They slowly began to kiss, to vanquish history and childish misunderstandings. To forgive each other and forge new beginnings. They'd already made a significant head start, but Diane couldn't help but wonder how anything would have changed if either one of them had not come to St. John for Christmas.

Hale made swift work of removing Diane's silk sheath. He cupped her breasts, massaging her extended nipples with his thumbs while his tongue danced with hers in a deeply erotic kiss. She was now stripped down to just a pair of black thong panties.

Hale began to undress as Diane removed the floral spread and stretched out on the bed on her back. She lay, intently watching as Hale tossed aside the black shirt and stepped out of his slacks and shorts together. He was at full magnificent extension, boldly displayed. When she raised her gaze to meet his, his eyes seemed stormy and clouded with passion. He wanted her as much as she wanted him.

Hale leaned forward at the end of the bed, bracing his hands and knee on the edge. He began skulking toward her, like a great cat about to ravish her. He straddled her hips, giving Diane the perfect opportunity to stroke and fondle him. He blindly searched for the lamp switch and turned off the lights, then lowered his body to lie full-length on top of her.

Hale made no attempt to remove her pants, and Diane writhed beneath him in frustration, having to settle for his bewitching kisses, the gyration of his hips and hard penis against her groin and his hands everywhere. He rolled off to the side and, still kissing her, slid a hand beneath the flimsy band of her panties and began to rub and stroke between her legs.

She gasped, letting out a heart-wrenching moan, and completely surrendered to his manipulations. All the while he was kissing her slowly, softly, teasingly. Diane felt invaded from top to bottom.

There was a knock on the door.

"Room service," a young male voice with an island lilt announced from the other side.

Hale continued administering to her as if he hadn't heard. The knock came again, and the announcement.

"H-Hale," she panted. "The…door…"

"What do you want?" he asked seductively. "The wine or this?"

Diane moaned again, her hands gripping the sheets. She ignored the summons to the door and turned her face into the pillow as she was overtaken with a throbbing paroxysm of pleasure.

Hale stared out over the spectacular vista. Even in the rain the landscape was lush and exotic. But the rain was finally slacking off and the sun was definitely breaking through. It was still early, but it was going to be another perfect day in paradise.

He smiled at the irony of his thoughts. It had been *nearly* perfect. The only "but" in his mind was what to expect once everyone left St. John for home. Maybe better not to think about that at the moment. *Enjoy what you have now*, he kept telling himself.

Why, when he'd already had every impossible dream realized? Why, then, did he feel like there was going to be a price to pay for his happiness?

The door slid open behind him and then closed again. He didn't move, but continued to stare at the muted gray colors produced by the rain. Finally, Diane stood behind him, her hands on his shoulders. She caressed them down his bare chest, leaning over to kiss the top of his head and then resting her chin there.

Hale reached up and took one of her hands, holding on…as if he was holding on to life itself.

"How'd you sleep?" he asked quietly.

"Sleep? I don't recall I got much of that."

"You complaining?"

She sighed, rubbed his chest, came around to position herself across his lap. She had only a plush white towel for cover, saronged around her body after her shower. She looped her arms around his neck and grinned at him.

"No. I'm not complaining, Hale. I was just thinking…"

She stopped and he waited, but she only shrugged shyly and shook her head, as if what she was thinking wasn't important. But he felt confident enough to guess what the unfinished thought was.

It was so nice to wake up in bed together.

Why couldn't she say it?

"I ordered breakfast."

"Oh, my God. You're wonderful." She sighed, kissing him briefly. "I'm starving."

Hale rubbed her shoulders, kissed her back. "I wonder why?"

She giggled. There was a knock at the door for room service. He stood, gently pushed her off his lap and entered the room to answer.

"Do you think it's the same man from last night? Give him the empty wine bottle," she called out.

Breakfast was wheeled in on a service cart with a snowy-white table cloth, several covered dishes, a carafe of coffee and pitchers of ice water and guava juice. There was also a bud vase holding one bird-of-Paradise stem. By the time the service had been set up on the glass table on the terrace, the rain had stopped completely and the sun miraculously broke through a drifting cloud with sudden heat and light.

Hale thought it best to keep breakfast conversation as general as possible. He admitted to himself that he didn't want to explore feelings, his or hers, about what the night before had meant to them. But they did talk about their night together. For Hale, although he kept this to himself, it was as he'd always imagined but never had a hope of actually experiencing. As for Diane, he knew nothing of her expectations. He only knew for sure what he wanted. Her. Always.

When breakfast was done they sat quietly, holding hands, totally peaceful. Hale recognized it was because they'd made an unspoken agreement to stay in the moment. It was easier this way.

"Happy New Year," he murmured, squeezing her hand and raising it to his lips for a kiss.

She sighed. "No, not yet. Tomorrow will be here soon enough. Tomorrow…"

"We go home."

"Yes," she murmured, pensive.

"Okay. How about, a very happy ending to the year?"

"Yes, I like that," Diane said.

Hale turned his attention to the sea. He'd settle for that ending. For now.

"I'm glad you came down for the holiday."

Diane smiled at her father as he turned her to the beat of the music. "I had a great time, Daddy. It was fun being with everyone."

"That include Hale?"

She felt a swirl of some emotion in her chest, but knew it was too late to pretend she and Hale were still circling around each other like adversaries. Spending the time she had with him had been a bonus. She wasn't going to deny it.

"Yes, including Hale. You know, I've grown up. I don't hold a grudge against him anymore."

"Forgive me for saying so, but you never should have in the first place. That said, I'm glad you two are getting along."

They maneuvered through the crowd of revelers on the dance floor of the Caneel Bay terrace restaurant. She caught a glimpse of Hale dancing with Courtney, and Simon standing and having a drink with Katie. Her eyes searched until she found Hayden, slouched in a chair talking with his mother. Bailey was flirting with a very cute server behind the hors d'oeuvre table.

Her father will not be amused, Diane considered, hoping Adam did not notice and take action.

"So, my next question is," he interrupted her thought, "what's going on with my wife?"

Diane missed a step, and her father smoothly led her back into the rhythm.

"What? What are you talking about?" she asked, frowning at him.

"That little ruse about going to see the cardiac facility at the health center didn't wash with me. They don't have one. If there's more than a routine problem with heart patients on St. John they're sent over to the Schneider Regional on St. Thomas, or maybe flown out to Puerto Rico."

Diane looked into her father's face. His calm questioning belied the pointed way he was studying her, and she knew he'd catch her in any lie. That's what parents do.

"Well, it's not like I really lied to you. I just didn't tell you everything."

"You can tell me now."

"It's okay, really. Eva was feeling uncomfortable and sort of knew it was a female thing. She wanted to talk to me about it. The fact that she hasn't said anything to you means there was nothing to tell."

"Full disclosure, Diane," he said firmly. "Tell me anyway."

He was not to be put off and she couldn't blame him. It was only more proof, as if she hadn't seen and heard enough in twenty years, of her father's love and devotion to Eva. Diane didn't want him to worry.

"I took her for a sonogram. It showed Eva might have some cysts, maybe a fibroid. I told her to see her GYN when you return home. Trust me on this, Daddy. It's not serious."

He listened intently and finally nodded, turning her again to the music. "Okay, if you say so."

"I say so. And don't say that I told you. More than anything, Eva doesn't want to worry you. Okay?"

"Okay," Adam said with a deep sigh. He looked into her eyes. "Have I told you how proud I am of you?"

"Not recently," she said coyly.

"Seriously. I'm glad Eva has you to turn to, Diane."

Diane smiled at her father, silently thanking him for such a lovely gift.

"I'll swap with you."

Diane and her father both were surprised by Hale's sudden appearance. He was partnering Eva. Diane watched as Adam gladly released her to take his wife in his arms, smiling down at her with love.

"Finally," he said as they danced away, disappearing into the other couples on the floor.

Diane gazed up at Hale as he took her in his arms. They had only danced together once since arriving at the party, and he'd been sure to get her for the slow number. He was smiling down at her and it struck her that he seemed the most relaxed and happy she'd ever seen him. Whatever her feelings may have been about Hale in the past, she had to accept that her parents considered him part of their family. They had known him almost half of his life. And there was no denying that there had been a big shift in her own feelings recently. Spending the holidays with him had been...

"You okay?" he asked, scanning her expression.

Diane forced herself to smile. "Hmm."

"Ten more minutes."

She blinked, trying to stay focused. "And then what?"

"Hello?" he chuckled. "What planet did you just

land from? Ten minutes and we're into a new year. Any resolutions?" he asked.

"No, I…I really haven't given it any thought," Diane murmured.

"I have," he said, his voice low and intimate. He held her a little tighter. "My resolution is to not look back on the past anymore. I can't change any of it. So, I'm focusing on the future."

"Can you be more specific?" she asked.

He seemed to be thinking about his answer. He finally shook his head, even though he also regarded her with a steady, warm gaze.

"Not yet."

The music suddenly stopped and there was a smattering of applause throughout the open terrace. Hale took her hand as they watched the final preparations for ringing in the new year.

Diane craned her neck to try and locate her family. Her father's height made him easy to spot, and she knew that Eva would be right next to him. She found Simon, Katie and Hayden, and finally Bailey and Courtney in the company of two young men. She had to remind herself that at sixteen they weren't doing anything she hadn't done at their age. Hopefully not everything, she thought, thinking of Hale.

Red, royal blue and purple party hats with the new year printed in silver or gold around the rim were stacked on tables for the guests to take. Noisemakers were being passed out by waitstaff carrying around large baskets. Champagne bottles were uncorked and poured glasses were set. A flat-screen TV had been temporarily brought in from the lounge and tuned to a station for the countdown in New York's Times Square.

"One minute to go!" the bandleader shouted, and everyone cheered again.

Hale stepped away briefly and grabbed glasses of champagne for them. Just for a moment as she stood by herself, Diane recalled the last two New Years Eve she'd spent alone by choice. The memory of Trevor walking out during the holiday still too prominent and painful for her to even think about celebrating. But she hadn't thought of that more than once or twice since arriving on the island. Not at all since she and Hale had...

"Remember, this is about letting go of the past."

Hale pressed a glass into her hand and they turned to listen to the countdown.

"Eight...seven...six..."

You make it sound so easy, Diane thought, but she couldn't ignore something her father and Eva, and even Hale himself, had said that was starting to really trouble her.

"Three...two...Onnneeeeeeee!"

Diane looked at Hale, and her heart did an unexpected flip-flop. It took her completely by surprise.

What was that?

Suddenly, from above, there was a sudden rain of colorful confetti and the waitstaff was throwing out streamers.

Hale put an arm around her and bent to kiss her. Her response was a little tentative and she knew it. When Hale pulled back Diane could see in his eyes that he felt it, too.

"Happy New Year," he said, watching her closely.

"You, too...."

Someone threw their arms around her neck, startling her.

"Happy New Year," Bailey said with great exuberance.

She was immediately followed by Hayden and Courtney and Eva and her father. A glance over her shoulder showed that Hale was getting similar treatment.

Diane felt herself enveloped in a bear hug.

"Well, we survived another year," Adam said over the noise.

"Yeah, we did. Daddy, you said that Hale used to work for a drug company."

He sighed, impatient. "Diane, give it a rest. What does it matter?"

She stared at him, waiting. He gave in.

"That's right, he did. Why?"

"Who does he work for now?"

Adam frowned. "You shouldn't have to ask me that, Diane."

"I know, but…please tell me."

Diane was aware that her father looked like he'd rather fall on a bed of nails than answer, but then he seemed to quickly get over his hesitancy.

"He still works for Carlyle. He's a lobbyist on the Hill for them."

Chapter 9

He wasn't fooled for a minute.

Hale could see that Diane was doing her best to appear as if nothing was wrong. But her body language, her refusal to meet his gaze, told a different story.

She'd fixed a placid and pleasant smile to her face all during the goodbyes with her family on the dock at Cruz Bay. They were staying for one more day to avoid the postholiday crowds of people returning home. He, Simon and Diane were headed back to the airport on St. Thomas to catch flights. He wasn't sure if anyone else noticed that Diane was distracted and distant. Particularly with him. Only Adam, shaking his hand and squeezing his shoulder murmuring, "Good luck," hinted at his awareness of Diane's sudden swift change of attitude.

For the life of him, Hale couldn't put his finger on anything specific that might have caused Diane to close down. Already he was sensing that, for whatever reason, they were back to first base. That the gains he and Diane had made together over the holiday were about to vanish into thin air.

The ferry was filled with people and luggage. She was seated very close to him, her shoulder and side pressed against him as people squeezed in on all sides for the twenty-minute ride. But she was not relaxed. And even as he stretched out an arm behind her along the top of the seat, he felt Diane was only pretending to be at ease.

"Hey, are you ever in the Boston area?"

Hale drew in a deep breath of frustration and gave Simon his attention.

"Never been to Boston."

"You have to come sometime. Be my guest. Me and Diane were raised just outside the city. Actually, just me. Diane's been raised all up and down the East Coast." Simon chuckled.

Hale glanced at her for her reaction, but she didn't appear to have even heard her brother's comment. He knew that after her father and mother divorced, both parents had remarried and started new families. He understood how she might have felt, being the only child having to shuttle back and forth growing up. That fact made it doubly annoying that she'd never understood his sense of displacement, of not having a place where he totally belonged.

"Thanks. I might just take you up on that."

"Listen, I can sometimes score tickets for the home games. I don't guess you're a Patriots or Celtics fan?"

"Man, I'm from D.C. If my team is playing your team, that could be worth a trip."

"Bet," Simon grinned, and they exchanged a knuckle bump.

"What about you, Diane? Diane?"

Hale lightly tapped her shoulder to get her attention. She jumped.

"What? Sorry, I didn't hear you," she said.

She looked, puzzled, between him and Simon, not even sure who had spoken. He watched her expression, picking up on the tightly drawn mouth, the slight furrow between her brows. Even the way she sat with her arms and legs crossed.

She had completely shut him out.

"I said, when are you coming up to Boston? Mom's going to ask."

She adjusted her sunglasses, moistened her lips. "I don't know. I have a lot on my agenda this month. Probably for her birthday in February."

"Call and let her know," Simon suggested. "I'm not delivering any messages."

Diane sighed and turned away impatiently. "Fine," she said shortly.

Hale exchanged exasperated looks with Simon.

There was the usual slow march through the check-in process at the airport, which also required clearing customs before passing through security. Given how the previous evening had ended, and the uncertain start to the first day of the year, Hale was glad that Simon was lively and filled with interesting observations and comments.

Despite Diane's assessment of Simon as the Golden Child who could do no wrong, at least where their mother was concerned, Hale liked him a lot. While it was clear to him that they didn't have a lot in common, Hale had no trouble with seeing the two of them as friends. So he was relieved that Simon, probably unknowingly, filled in the awkward gaps and silences left by Diane's failure to engage.

But the truth be known, Hale was anxious to talk with her. To find out what the problem was. Had she received news about a patient in D.C.? Was she just tired from a holiday of nonstop activities…including a deeply gratifying series of time together when they made love? Did it have to do with her father and Eva? Or was it all about him?

They announced Simon's flight to Boston, and Hale was glad that Diane could rouse herself sufficiently to say goodbye to her brother. They walked him to the gate, and they could see his plane boarding on the tarmac beyond the plate glass windows.

"Great to meet you, man," Simon said, unexpectedly giving him a brief handshake and chest bump. "Don't forget my offer. It's real."

"Thanks. I appreciate it."

"Big Sis." He grinned at Diane.

Diane blinked, as if realizing that he was really leaving. "I'm so glad you made it." She and Simon hugged each other tightly with warmth and love.

"Me, too. Love you."

With a cheerful wave he gave the attendant his boarding pass and walked through the open door to the waiting plane.

Hale watched Diane watching her brother leave. She stared after him a long time and he suspected she was thinking the same thing he was. Now it was just the two of them.

Finally, she turned to look him in the face. The first time she'd done so all day. He knew his gaze was filled with questions and surprise. Doubt.

She broke their gaze and simply walked away, back to the seating area near their gate.

"Okay, enough," Hale said, standing in front of her, looking down at her aloof expression.

She stiffened and even people sitting nearby grew quiet at his hard tone.

"Talk to me," Hale said, louder and firmer than he'd meant to. But he would do whatever was necessary to get a response from her.

She jumped up from her seat. "People are staring."

"Let them. This could get worse. I could really give them something to talk about."

Several people snickered nervously, many others were nervously silent but paying attention.

Her eyes narrowed, taking his threat to heart. Better. Now he had her attention.

"Let it go."

"You're kidding, right? You started this. You've been treating me like I eat dirt since last night. I want to know what I've done now to offend you."

He didn't realize how angry he'd become over the last twelve hours until that moment. People were moving, changing seats, getting out of the line of fire. He could detect several blue-shirted airport agents, standing in his peripheral vision, watching.

He could see he'd embarrassed her. Her eyes were stormy. He was momentarily taken with how beautiful Diane was in her anger. She got in his face, her voice low and tight.

"You work for a company that should be put out of business. They promote drugs that aren't considered safe, and they sell drugs to people who don't need them."

Hale stared blankly at her. For a full minute he had no idea what she was talking about.

"I took away two different prescriptions from my stepmother made by *your* company that might have done real damage to her. I know that Carlyle is not considered an honest company. How can you actually work for them? Are they paying you so much money that it doesn't matter to you?"

Her voice began to rise in her righteous indignation. He could hear the silence in the waiting area. The whole room was still and no one moved. Two of the agents were slowing walking their way. Raising his hand, he briefly signaled that there would be no need for them to intervene.

Hale tightened his jaw and clamped down on his teeth. If he answered right away he knew it would be a knee-jerk reaction. He'd be striking back to hurt her, how she was hurting him in ways she didn't even realize. Or maybe she did. He wasn't going to tell her off the way he might have when he was nineteen and she'd attacked him with equally uncalled for accusations. He wasn't going to go back to the old ways.

If he wasn't careful he'd lose everything.

"Diane, you don't know squat about me or what I do. You never did. You never took the time to find out because you wanted to believe I was *never* going to be good enough. It's unforgivable that you believe I would do anything to hurt Eva. She and Adam have been good to me. Maybe better than I deserved in the beginning, but they never lost faith in me and I've never let them down."

"Why didn't you tell me about Carlyle?"

"I don't owe you an explanation about Carlyle," he bit out, stabbing a finger at her. She flinched.

"Keep it down, sir, or I'll have to ask you to leave the terminal."

Hale took a deep breath. He glanced at the agents and nodded.

"Carlyle is…is despicable."

"You're right. They were. That's why I quit working for them. Let's get something else straight. Don't blame me for mistakes made by doctors like you. It's your responsibility to make sure your patients are getting the right medication, not lawyers like me! You expect me to believe you've never given a patient a sample drug to try that was given you by some pharma rep?"

Diane opened her mouth to retaliate, but froze. She seemed to be struggling to find words.

He wasn't about to let up.

"What you're trying to pin on me I don't do to people I care about. People I've come to love," Hale said, his voice low and firm with emphasis. She gazed at him, but quickly shifted her eyes away. "I owe your father my life. I owe Eva much more, because she was good to me and kind and sweet. Unlike you."

"Maybe I just see things differently than Eva," Diane said, the energy leaving her words.

It sounded like a weak strike.

"I hoped that would change but…" Hale sighed, suddenly tired and dispirited. He shook his head, pensive. "This Christmas was…more than I could ever have hoped for. Being on St. John with your whole family…feeling like I was part of it. It was real nice." He looked long and hard at her. "Feeling like, maybe you and I…"

Her gaze shot back to his. Wide and questioning, waiting for him to continue. But he thought better of it.

He wasn't going to expose his belly and give her another opportunity to attack.

"Maybe I was wrong about Carlyle, but Daddy said you're a lobbyist for a drug company. That's not much better, is it?"

Closing his eyes warily, Hale shook his head and began to back away from her. He raised his arms in surrender.

"That's it. I'm down for the count. You don't know what's true, and I don't feel like helping you figure it out. I'm not doing this anymore, Diane. You win."

Hale turned, found his seat and picked up his computer case. Pulling out his boarding pass he walked to the ticket agent's desk. He had no idea what Diane was doing but he had no intention of turning around to find out. He was afraid that he might go back on his own word.

Slowly, conversation was picking up again in the waiting area. It was as if everyone had simultaneously let out their breaths in relief that the unbelievable public scene they'd all witnessed was over.

The attendant was professional and cool, acting as if she and her colleagues had not heard every word of the showdown.

"Sorry about that," Hale felt compelled to say.

"No problem, sir. How can I help you?"

"I need a big favor. I changed my seat assignment by phone two days ago, but I don't think it's a good idea that I'm next to the lady. Any chance you can help a brother out again and find me a new seat?"

She took his pass, giving him what Hale read as an understanding glance.

"I'm sure I can find something for you."

* * *

Diane absently swept her fingers through her hair, doing more harm than good. She quietly bid good-night to colleagues she passed in the corridor as she headed toward her office. She shared the small space with another physician and when she entered the room she was relieved to see that he'd already left for the day. She was about to close herself in when someone on the other side pushed the door open again.

"Sorry…I thought you'd want to see this before you leave."

The nurse held out a patient folder to her. Diane stared at it before taking it, already suspecting that it was a case that might require her to stay late at the clinic.

"What is it?"

"It's about a boy named Que…Qua…"

"Oh, yes. Qa'Shawn Davis." She took the folder. "Thanks. Anything unusual?"

"Not according to the echo or EKG."

Diane began reading the machine records from both tests as she blindly made her way to her desk and sat down. After reviewing the reports twice she placed a call and sat back in her chair, her eyes momentarily closed. She felt bone-tired. She hadn't slept well for weeks and it was beginning to take a toll. She was exhausted and tense and sad.

"Ron here. What can I do for you?"

Diane sat forward and forced herself to sound alert and confident.

"Hi, Ron. It's Diane Maxwell."

"Hey. Dr. Diane. How goes it? I hope you're calling to tell me you can give me two or three hours next week to check out some new cases."

"I wish I could, but I'm still trying to catch up from

being away over Christmas. I do have good news for you. I got the test results for Qa'Shawn."

"We can always use good news around here."

"He's fine. Like I said, that murmur is very common with children. He's a skinny kid, so his heart lies close to his chest, and when you examine him you can hear the flow of blood. It's called a functional murmur."

"Meaning?"

"There's no heart disease. He'll probably outgrow it. There's no need to restrict his activities."

"Good, because he's incapable of sitting still."

Diane grinned. "That means he's really a very normal little boy. You might want to have me or someone check him a year from now, to see if there's any change. I don't think there will be."

"Sounds like a plan, but I can't guarantee where Qa'Shawn and his mother will be a year from now. Could find them a real place to live. Or they could end up at another shelter."

"Oh. I'm sorry to hear that. The families at your shelter are just trying to make it day to day."

"It's hard."

"Well...you know, I think I can come by and give you some time."

"You sure?"

"I'll make it happen."

Ron laughed. "You're a good woman, Dr. Diane."

She laughed. "There are some who wouldn't agree with you."

"I should have told you you're on speakerphone. I have someone in my office. Hale Cameron. You remember him, right?"

Diane's stomach did an alarming sudden drop. She felt both overwhelmingly hot and nauseous. She knew she wasn't ill. It was the tension. Every time she heard Hale's name, and had a total recall of the time they'd been together on St. John, her body betrayed her and tied her stomach into knots.

"Yes. I remember him," she said with as little emotion as she could manage.

"I can always count on you and Hale. He just dropped off a couple of our teens after a Take-Our-Kids-To-Work day. Hale doesn't have any kids, and most of the kids here have no fathers. But he offered to show them what he does. I think he found a future attorney or two." Ron cackled.

"That...that's really great," she said enthusiastically. Her heart was thumping in her chest. "Listen, I really have to run, and I don't want to take up your time with... Hale. I'll bring over a copy of Qa'Shawn's record when I come next week."

"Thanks for everything, Diane. You're the greatest."

Hale doesn't think so, she thought, ending the call. She sat holding the cordless in her hands.

She couldn't blame him.

All her sleepless nights, all the rehashing and second-guessing about what happened at the airport on St. Thomas and, worse, the look of defeat and disappointment in his eyes when he'd walked away from her, clearly spoke of someone who didn't care anymore.

Her stomach roiled. She pressed her arm across her stomach...and prayed for a swift end to her agony.

You win.

That's what Hale had said. But what, she asked herself constantly, had she won? To be right? To put him down…or in his place? To be free of him? Is that what she wanted?

Diane groaned and jumped out of her chair as if it had gotten too hot.

I thought that you and I…

Diane covered her face with her hands and blindly began to pace the confines of the small office. She bumped into a chair, her foot kicked the wastepaper basket, the noise startling her.

I thought you and I…

She stopped and collapsed on the edge of her desk, bent over with her head drooping.

She needed to talk to someone. The list of anyone who would empathize with her was very short, but only because she couldn't clearly articulate what was wrong. Except she felt terrible. And sick.

Diane turned around to reach for the phone again. Maybe Eva or her father. No. Not Adam. Her father had already made his thoughts known on everything Hale and her, and the events of the holidays on St. John. As a matter of fact, when the subject had come up, just a few days after she'd returned to D.C. and had already had second thoughts on the way she'd handled that episode at the airport, she'd gotten no sympathy from her father. If anything, he'd seemed deeply disappointed in her.…

"Okay, first things first. Don't even try to convince me that there's nothing between you and Hale."

"There isn't. By the time we left St. John everything was back to normal," Diane had confessed.

"That part I get, too. The day you left the island you could have cut the tension between you two with a knife. What's going on? I thought you and Hale had finally worked things out after all these years of squaring off with each other."

"I don't know what you mean," Diane had muttered, letting the dinner her father was treating her to sit and go cold. She hadn't felt much like eating, either.

"Look, baby, I *know* you and I know Hale. From where I stood it seemed like something pretty good going on. You seemed happy. Relaxed. We didn't hear word one about Trevor and two years ago."

"Well, you're wrong."

Her father had narrowed his gaze at her. "Oh. We're back to that again. When are you going to stop treating the man like he's done something reprehensible and you can't stand him? 'Cause I don't believe that's the issue."

"Daddy, don't. Please stay out of it."

Adam had sighed, looking both helpless and annoyed with her. He had shaken his head.

"You're going to blow this. You're too stubborn to realize Hale's your equal, in every way."

"Stay out of this!" She had stopped abruptly and clamped her mouth shut. She had realized she was drawing attention in the restaurant.

Adam had ignored the outburst and had looked at her sternly.

"I'm your father. I can see what's going on because you're just like me. You get hurt by someone or something, or *think* that someone has done you wrong, and you're like a wounded animal. Get over it, baby. Or you're going to be sorry...."

You're going to be sorry....

Diane moaned, then started when the phone rang. She stared at it. It rang a second time. A large part of her wondered at the possibility of it being Hale. But why would it be, after all the terrible things she'd accused him of and after what he'd said to her. It rang a third time and she picked it up.

"Diane Maxwell."

"It's Eva, honey."

She didn't know if she was relieved or disappointed. "Hi, Eva. I was just thinking about you."

"Really?"

"I was going to call you…."

And cry on your shoulder.

"About what?"

Diane shrugged, trying to make up something quickly. "Oh, just to say hello. See how you're feeling. I did want to find out if you've been to see your doctor since returning home."

"That's what I'm calling about myself. Well, they did another sonogram and confirmed what they found on St. John. The cysts will disappear on their own. They're not a problem. But the fibroids…the bottom line is there are actually two, one behind the other." She chuckled. "I gave your father a good scare. I was beginning to look three or four months pregnant."

"Your doctor wants to operate," Diane guessed succinctly.

"Yes. The fibroids are pushing and crowding some of my vital organs and my doctor isn't happy about that. Adam and I talked about it, and I'm going ahead with surgery in February."

"That's a good idea. What method have you and the doctor agreed on?"

Diane was grateful for a chance to clear her mind and talk on a subject she knew very well. Medicine. She felt better, professional, being able to offer advice and support to her stepmother. They talked about her father's response to the upcoming surgery and, of course, Adam had more questions for the doctors than Eva herself. Diane smiled at the image of her father grilling some unsuspecting GYN about the care of his wife.

"Have you heard about Hale?" Eva asked.

Diane was alert again. It was a simple enough question and didn't sound as if Eva was fishing for information.

"What about him?"

"I know your father told you Hale is a lobbyist. Now, I know what people think about lobbyists, but Hale is different. Really. Anyway, he's been invited to speak as a rep for a committee investigating drug companies, before a congressional hearing. He was asked for his opinion after talking to some of the bigwigs on the Hill about some of the ongoing problems. Can you believe it? Our Hale!"

"That's impressive," Diane said, her voice flat with shock.

Eva gave her the date, still exclaiming like a proud mama. As well she should, Diane conceded. Eva always knew that Hale would do himself proud.

All Diane could feel in that moment of Eva's excitement was overwhelmed. Empty. And sorry for herself.

That night she had the dream again but it was slightly different. She knew the heat of passion was going to rise within her, possibly consume her with need and the desire to be satisfied with him. That was both the delicious and frustrating part of the night. Then he'd whispered to her, but the words had gotten lost and faded in the act of her awaking.

Diane lay trying to reconstruct that moment. Putting the sounds together and the words and the meaning.

To imagine he'd said something like *I love you* was just wishful thinking.

Diane took her bag from the plastic bin that had just been passed through the scanning machine at the public entrance to the building. She was directed to an elevator and boarded along with a dozen other people, headed to one committee meeting or another in the House. Once off the elevator, she began walking in the direction of the room assigned to the hearing on health and families.

From the moment she'd made the decision and pursued the arrangements to attend the hearing, she had been filled with anxiety. A few times she'd thought better of the idea, afraid of the message it might send to her parents, or even Hale if he got wind of it. But mostly, she was afraid of what she was telling herself about finally wanting to hear Hale speak for himself.

But it was also that anxiety and inability to find peace, day to day, that forced her to recognize some hard truths not only about Hale and how terribly she'd misjudged him, but also about herself. The picture that was painted was not pretty.

Her heart racing, Diane took a deep breath and walked with purpose and her head high as she reached the hearing chamber. Someone took her ticket for the event and checked her name on a list and asked her to turn off her cell phone. They might have taken it from her until the hearing was over, until she identified herself as a doctor.

Beyond the last line of security Diane spotted a woman standing in the corridor along the wall. She looked familiar and Diane approached her. The young woman, petite and smartly dressed, seemed uncertain about going into the hearing chamber.

"Hi. Jenna?"

The young woman stared at her, momentarily puzzled, and then she smiled.

"Hi. You're Hale's friend, Diane."

"How are you?" Diane asked, ignoring Jenna's reference. "How's the baby?"

"Oh, he's great. He's with a sitter today. But he's getting so big." She beamed.

"I bet. Are you here for the hearing?"

"Yes. You, too?"

Diane nodded. "As a doctor I'm curious to hear what Hale has to say about upcoming legislation on the drug company issues."

Jenna made a face. "He'd like to cut their you-know-what off, not that he's really said that. You know Hale's been on the inside so he knows what he's talking about. He wants the companies to be responsible for their dirty tricks. And he wants them to pay."

Diane raised her brows, a little amused by the young woman's vehemence. "You seem to know a lot about it."

"Well, I'm almost finished with my nursing degree so I've heard and seen a lot where I'm working now.

"I got some really good news that Colby may be coming home by June," Jenna said, changing the subject on a dime.

Her excitement was palpable, her eyes bright with love and anticipation.

"That's really great news. I'll keep my fingers crossed for you."

"You ladies will have to go in if you're here for the hearing."

"Hale doesn't know I'm here. I had to beg a coworker to change days with me," Jenna confided in a whisper as they walked together into the chamber and were directed to seats.

"He doesn't know I'm here, either," Diane confessed.

The preliminaries, while interesting to witness, only served to draw out Diane's nervousness until her hands were icy cold and her body was stiff with tension. She didn't see Hale among the people already seated, and didn't want to appear gauche by turning her head every time someone entered the room. People continued to file in. Then another door opened into the chamber on the other side of the room. A number of men and two women entered single file and took seats in the front row behind a long balustrade. Hale was the third person in.

Diane's stomach did what it had been doing for weeks. Twisting and turning, even more so, now that she was seeing Hale for the first time since that last horrible time they were together. She couldn't take her eyes from him. Like that night she'd seen him at the gala in Baltimore. He looked incredibly handsome in his dark business suit. He moved, tall and imperial, with a walk that still had a hint of a swagger.

Her heart seemed to ache in her chest and, unconsciously, she placed a hand over to soothe it.

Diane watched as the announcements were made about the purpose of the hearing, naming the committee members and the invited expert speakers. Hale leaned in to catch the comments of another speaker, an elderly woman, seated next to him. As he turned his head to whisper a response he happened to glance over the woman's shoulder and his gaze met hers.

There was no mistaking the surprise in his eyes. Diane sat stunned as she decided what to do. Should she smile? Wave? Nod encouragement? She was not given a chance to do anything.

"I think he saw us," Jenna murmured softly.

Well, what did you expect?

The hearing was about a committee of the House that proposed legislation that did more than go after drug companies who blatantly disregarded rules and regulations of the FDA, solely in the pursuit of profits while putting the health of citizens at risk. The committee wanted to raise the already steep fines imposed on companies found guilty, and they wanted prosecutors to be able to go after doctors who accept kickbacks from companies to promote and prescribe their drugs.

When Hale took the mic to give his presentation, Diane sat riveted. He was authoritative and he was courageous in talking about how he came to know Carlyle Pharmaceuticals. Hale admitted working for them fresh out of law school, the high pay and benefits seductive and hard to turn down. After several years he put together a true picture of how the company operated and why the profits were so high. He quit and, on behalf of a group of poorly served people, filed a class action and sued the company.

Carlyle lost the case and was forced to pay billions in retribution. Hale's case also caused the company to nearly go bankrupt, until the CEO was forced out and the company was under new leadership. It was now known as Medpro. The new company has a better vision and believes in their mission, Hale said, to provide quality and safe medications to the millions of people whose lives depend on them. The company hired Hale back to work for them, and their new commitment, on the Hill in D.C. as a lobbyist.

The information left Diane feeling numb. And very stupid. She hadn't known, and she could have found out. She could have had the information before she made the unfounded accusations she had against Hale.

She'd ruined everything and for no reason. Except, maybe, fear.

His presentation was flawless and even under questioning from the panel afterward, he never faltered and answered every question with facts, statistics, anecdotes, sometimes throwing the questions back at the panel members, much to the amusement of the attendees, who chuckled or laughed at the attempts to trip Hale in his logic or argument.

The hearing lasted two hours. By the time the panel adjourned Diane was exhausted, as if she had endured the same cross-fire. She had, but it was self-imposed.

They filed out of the chamber, the crowd meandering toward the bank of elevators.

"I've got to get back," Jenna said, frowning. "Time to pump or I'm going to start leaking."

Diane chuckled. "It was nice to see you again."

"Yeah, same here. Maybe I can have you and Hale for dinner one night. If you don't mind the baby fussing for my attention."

She encouraged Jenna to squeeze on to the first elevator available. The elevators were slow and even more people gathered as the committee room emptied. Two arrived at once, the bell indicator dinging at the same time. She boarded and turned to face the front. Diagonally across from her some of the hearing speakers were just getting on the other elevator, laughing and chatting now that it was over. Hale was in the middle, entering the elevator and facing front.

Across the distance between the two elevators they,

once again, stared at each other. But there was no time for Diane to assess that moment. She left the building feeling that it may possibly be the last time she'd ever see Hale.

It was just after ten when Hale entered his apartment, cold and tired. Winter had never been his favorite time of year, and between the weather and the last four weeks of preparing for the hearing, not eating right if at all and thinking about the end of the Christmas holidays, he was also not in a particularly good mood. Crappy would be the right word.

But somehow he'd dealt with it. What were the options? That is, until looking out into the viewing audience and seeing Diane seated next to Jenna at the hearing that morning.

He hadn't expected either one of them to be there, but it was Diane's presence that had had the greater effect. After seeing her he redoubled his efforts to concentrate and make his presentation knowing she was sitting behind him. The hearing had gone well, and he was pleased by the congratulations he'd received from two of the panelists for being prepared and answering their questions.

Hale put down his computer case, shrugged out of his wool coat and just left it with the scarf over the arm of his sofa. He frowned as he looked absently through his small stack of mail and then carelessly tossed it onto the coffee table. The thought *stiff drink* came to mind, but instead he went to his kitchen to get a can of beer from the refrigerator. He popped the tab and began sipping as he slowly made his way back to the living room to sit in the dark and once again conjure up the image of Diane as she'd appeared that morning.

God, she looked great.

Seeing her had felt like a stab to the chest, just when he thought the hole there was starting to heal. His heart had been pierced again, bleeding emotion and pain and loss. Why did Diane have to show up like that? Yet he was so glad she did. If for no other reason than it proved to him he was in no way, shape or form over her.

In that case, what the hell was he supposed to do?

The phone rang and Hale cursed it. He let it ring. And ring. And ring. Cursing still, he reached impatiently for the cordless but not in time. The answering machine clicked on and he sat back warily to hear the message. Fine. He didn't feel like talking to anyone right now, anyway.

Beeeeeep...

"Hi. It's Diane."

His stomach roiled and he stiffened with his second shock of the day. He leaned forward with his arms braced on his thighs. He closed his eyes to try and see her. He listened closely to her words. He could have picked up then but didn't. Couldn't.

"I...well, I know you saw me at the hearing. I hope you didn't mind. I...I heard about it from Eva and... well, I just decided to come.

"I knew I owed it to myself and to you to learn more about what it is you do, exactly. Better late than never, huh?"

He knew she chuckled just then, nervously. Then she sighed.

"I...eh...I wanted to say it was a real pleasure to hear the way you got right in the face of the drug companies. You were...awesome. I'm so glad I was there. Really. And..."

Hale heard her pause for a few long seconds.

"And I wanted to say I'm not a coward. I was prepared to say all this to you if you'd answered the phone. And I wouldn't have blamed you if you'd hung up on me. I deserve it. But I'm glad you're not home. Okay, so maybe I am a coward. If you had hung up on me I would have... well...anyway...I'm glad I came today, Hale. It was good to see you again. Bye."

Click.

Chapter 10

She could hear the music being spun by the DJ as she rode up the escalator. At the top the scene opened to a very long and wide expanse of brightly patterned carpeting, the kind typical of large chain hotels. There were at least a dozen small groups of men and women standing around in conversation with one another. The muted sounds of recorded music could just be heard beyond the closed doors of the ballroom.

Diane swiftly made her way to the coat check, accepting the claim ticket and dropping it into her purse. She sighed in relief as she glanced quickly around to double-check how the women were dressed, just to make sure that the evening had not called for formal wear. She'd learned the hard way that winter weather was not conducive to comfort in strapless gowns and skimpy sandals. But the occasion tonight was not formal. Merely a professional gathering of young

Washingtonians, the purpose of which was to provide networking opportunities for many who, in one way or another, worked in D.C. with or for various government agencies. As a new member of an advocacy group for family health, this was her first time at such an event.

Not knowing a soul was the hard part about coming to these events. Diane suspected that from the number of milling people outside, and the fast dance music inside, that there could easily be several hundred people here.

"Hi, I'm Sheila Matthews."

Diane turned to the cheerful greeting and found a bespectacled woman smiling at her. The woman thrust out her hand.

"I'm with the events committee. Is this your first time here?"

"Yes, it is." Diane returned the smile and shook the woman's hand. "Diane Maxwell."

"Welcome, Diane. It's nice to have you with us this evening. Here's information on upcoming events and programs for the spring."

Diane accepted a single sheet folded in half that was laid out and printed with a long list.

"As you can hear, the reception is in full swing. Please go on in. Introduce yourself and have a great evening."

The woman smiled again but quickly moved on to other people arriving behind her.

Clutching the paper, Diane slowly walked through the door that was being held for her by an attendant. The music inside was actually not much louder than what leaked out into the corridor. It actually served more as background noise, as no one inside was actually dancing.

She began aimlessly walking through the room with

lots more people than she thought would attend. And everyone really seemed to be enjoying themselves. Everyone seemed to know someone, who then introduced them to someone else. That's the way these events were meant to work.

There were three open bar stations and she maneuvered her way through the crowds toward one of them. She exchanged brief polite greetings and smiles in passing with any number of people, and soon she was stopped by a man who recognized her from a cardiology symposium they'd both attended a year earlier. He reintroduced himself and, with relief, Diane realized she was now in the mix. Before very long someone else joined them who simply said hello and began a conversation. What she was particularly relieved about was that she had no sense that the conversation was a come-on from either man. And, as it turned out, one of them was waiting for his wife to arrive.

Soon the acquaintance excused himself because he saw someone else he knew. The three of them quickly exchanged business cards, and Diane took that moment to continue her journey to the bar.

Not so bad, she thought and sighed, encouraged.

She stood in line to get a glass of white wine. She was opening her wallet to pull out a bill to pay for it when a familiar voice broke through to her.

"Let me."

Diane turned and found Hale standing at her side. She stared openmouthed at him as he accepted the glass of wine from the bartender and handed the man a bill, waving away any change.

"Over here." He nodded and moved through the crowd to a tall, unoccupied table.

Diane followed, feeling oddly like a child obeying

the command of a knowledgeable adult. Fortunately the few moments it took for them to reach the stand and for Hale to set down the glass gave her the time she needed to pull her wits about her.

"Thank you," Diane said graciously, proud of her command of her tongue and the English language.

But then, for another few moments they simply looked at one another. Hale's gaze was steady and totally unfazed by seeing her. Diane, on the other hand, couldn't understand why she was blinking, and she seemed reluctant to look him directly in the face.

"Surprise," she said, a little breathless, taking a sip of the wine. "I didn't expect to see you here."

"I know. You never do. I saw you come in. You're late again."

She finally glanced at him and, although his face was still and blank of any particular emotion, Hale's eyes seemed friendly. She chuckled nervously. But she hadn't missed his reference to her past assumptions about him.

"Bad habit. I really have to do something about that. But I didn't get lost," she quickly added with a certain degree of pride. "The GPS you gave me got me here."

Hale nodded. "I thought you might have tossed it in a closet somewhere."

"No, of course not," she hastened to say. "It was one of the best gifts I got from Christmas."

This time she did brave a look at him and felt less apprehensive. She didn't see any anger or aloofness. She took another sip of wine, annoyed by her sense of intimidation. But it wasn't Hale's fault. It was her own.

"Have you...eh...been to these affairs before?"

Hale nodded. "A few. I never stay long. I know some people. First time I've seen you here."

"First time," she said, looking around. "I learned about the group and joined."

"I got the phone message."

Diane swallowed and looked at him. "Good. I wanted to say something."

"To say I was surprised to see you at the hearing is an understatement."

She sighed, nodding. "I know. But to be honest I felt I owed you that, and the respect of understanding what you do. And why. You handled yourself so well. It was a great presentation."

"I appreciate that," Hale said quietly.

She panicked, wondering why it was so hard to find the right things to say to him.

"Eva gave me her tickets. I hope that was okay. I'm not even sure how one gets tickets to official hearings."

"Ask your representative."

"Of course. That makes sense," she said wryly. "I'll know for next time. Will you…eh…be speaking again?"

"If I'm asked to. D.C. politics is not pretty. It's a system of favors, special interests and who you know. Trying to get elected officials to do right is not easy, unfortunately. So, I'll keep at it until I get at least Medpro recognized for being consumer-minded. A rare thing these days."

Diane listened attentively to what Hale was saying, impressed by his thinking, admiring his commitment.

"Then they're lucky to have you. Kids like Qa'Shawn at Ron's shelter are lucky to have you."

He nodded. "I know Qa'Shawn."

He wasn't making it easy for her, but Diane knew full

well it was not his responsibility. She accepted that any open lines of communication were all up to her. And she felt pleased that she and Hale were talking, having a conversation. Respecting one another...behaving like adults.

It could have been like this all along. Even better.

"Adam said that Eva might have some surgery?" Hale questioned, his expression now showing genuine concern and interest.

Diane smiled confidently. "Yes, but it's not serious. You know, doctors used to dismiss it, calling it 'a female thing.' It's not complicated and she'll only be in the hospital overnight. I'd tell you if it was anything else, Hale. I know how much Eva means to you."

"Thanks."

"Look...I was just wondering if..."

"There you are. I thought I was going to have to call your cell phone to locate you."

A tall black woman, beautifully dressed in an office-to-evening suit, appeared next to Hale. Diane found that she had to instantly appear calm, polite, professional and as if her hopes hadn't just taken a nosedive. She made sure she didn't turn a questioning gaze to Hale. After all, he owed her no explanation.

"I'm Dr. Diane Maxwell," she said graciously, extending her hand in greeting as another woman had done earlier for her.

"Have I seen you before?" the woman asked, taking her hand.

"This is Diane's first reception. She just joined."

"Oh, how nice. We're an interesting group, if I do say so myself."

Diane chuckled but she was aware that Hale was studying her closely.

"I'm Jill Weston."

"Jill is another of the counsels at Medpro. Diane is a friend of mine. We go way back."

Diane felt foolishly grateful to Hale for identifying her as a friend. But it did nothing to stem the sudden sinking of her spirits as she saw the way Jill positioned herself very closely next to Hale. Their arms were touching. Her repeated gazing into his face.

Then Hale turned to Jill with raised brows.

She chuckled. "Yes, I'm ready to leave. Diane, it was nice to meet you. Sorry to run out just as you've arrived. Maybe we'll see each other at a future event."

"Maybe," Diane said.

"I'm glad you came. Good night," Hale said quietly, before turning away to follow Jill through the crowd to the exit.

Diane wondered where they were headed together. The evening was young.

"Good night," she finally managed, dazed.

I'm glad you came....

Still, she felt like she might as well have been biding Hale goodbye.

Diane finished consulting with the attending nurse and then stepped back into the room where her stepmother had been taken, post op. An hour ago Eva had come to long enough to see Adam and her children briefly, before the doctor had advised letting her rest. She was going to be released the next morning and the family would have her back soon enough.

Diane sat in one of the visitor's chairs staring thoughtfully at Eva as she slept, while also feeling envious of the way her father had hovered over his wife, whispering to her with so much love. It was a sweet and poignant moment and the image stayed with her…as she thought of Hale.

"Are they gone?" Eva's voice suddenly slurred from the bed.

Diane quickly leaned forward and reached for the limp hand Eva attempted to raise. Diane clasped it, rubbing the back of the hand.

"Yes. Once the kids knew you're going home tomorrow, they wanted to go eat."

"Good. Now…you go…"

"I can stay a little longer…" Diane began, but then realized that Eva had once again fallen to sleep. With a light kiss on her stepmother's forehead she quietly left the room. The surgery had gone well and it only remained for Eva to recover and get her strength back.

She wasn't at all surprised to find Hale in the waiting room and she wondered how long he'd been sitting, alone. He was seated, staring down at his entwined hands with deep concentration, not aware of her presence.

She looked at him with newfound consideration. With an insight that perhaps had come too late. With longing. He glanced up, his brow clearing and his expression controlled.

"How is she?"

"Eva's fine. You missed my father. He just left to take Bailey and Hayden home."

Hale stood, looking at her. "I know. I passed them coming in. He said you stayed at the house last night so you could come with Eva when she checked in this morning. I told him I'd take care of you getting home."

She hid her surprise. "I don't mind calling a car service."

"Have you eaten anything today?" he asked, as if she hadn't spoken at all.

"Eat? I can't remember. I guess I did."

"Come on. Let's take it one step at a time."

Diane retrieved her coat from the nurses' station and she and Hale made their way to the hospital exit. As she walked beside him her thoughts were completely on trying to figure out what other steps Hale had in mind. Where exactly did they go from here? And she wasn't thinking about merely leaving the hospital.

It was a cold clear evening and their breath vaporized in the air as they walked to his car. His coat was open and his gloves were stuffed in the pockets. He had a scarf that coordinated with his coat wrapped twice around his throat and knotted. She was freezing, but he seemed so vigorous. There was something so strong and masculine about the way he'd just taken over and was making all the decisions.

She was so glad.

He even held the door for her and made sure she was comfortably seated before closing it and coming around to the driver side. And all the while she was remembering that testy time, months ago, when she'd last been with Hale in his car. When she'd wickedly misconstrued his relationship with Jenna…and he'd kissed her senseless.

Was that going to happen again?

She paid absolutely no attention to where they were headed, deep in thought and daydreaming, and just for the moment relieved not to have to make any more decisions, for herself or anyone else. She didn't mind the quiet between them, and it didn't seem the least bit uncomfortable.

It gave her time, as well, to reflect on that wonderful

time with Hale on St. John. It had happened so spontaneously, had been such a surprise.

"Where are we?" she asked suddenly, puzzled.

"U Street. This is where I live."

She said nothing, but watched the passing street scenes outside the window with interest. She knew that U Street, a historic and previously rundown black community, had been undergoing gentrification for a number of years. It was becoming a desirable destination for dining and the music scene, and tours of historic theaters and clubs. New upscale housing had been going up, drawing to it professional blacks looking to be part of the history and the future of the neighborhood. She had heard great things about the rebirth of U Street, and they all seemed to be true.

Hale drove off the main drag, however, and down a narrow street of smaller cafés and restaurants. He parked his car and escorted her inside one establishment. The interior was intimate. A pianist played light jazz to the side, but it didn't interfere with or take over conversation. There were maybe ten tables, and someone Diane presumed to be the manager or owner greeted Hale warmly. They were seated at one of two remaining vacant tables that secluded them in a corner, which was just fine with her.

For a long while they talked about the neighborhood, Diane asking questions of genuine interest and Hale easily responding, through drinks and shared appetizers. By the time they ordered dinner they had moved on to more questions about his work as a lobbyist and her volunteer time at the shelter that Ron managed. It also came up that she was leaving soon for two weeks in Africa, as part of a U.S. group of Doctors Without Borders initiative.

He was momentarily quiet when she revealed that information.

"Sounds a little dangerous."

Diane shrugged. "What isn't? I like being part of it. It reminds me of how lucky I am. I sometimes forget that."

He continued to watch her.

"When do you leave?"

"In early March. Why?"

"That's very soon," he murmured.

"Yes, it is."

By the end of dinner they'd finally eased into the subject they'd been avoiding. Or rather, she'd been avoiding. The truth. Her feelings about Hale. Her being in love with him. Admitting it, even to herself, seemed to have lifted a weight from her shoulders. But the bigger question was what to do about it. And was it too late?

"Would you like dessert?" Hale asked.

"No, I'll pass."

"Coffee?"

"It's late. I'm afraid it might keep me up."

He looked long and hard at her. "I doubt it."

She returned the long and hard look. "What do you mean?"

"I mean…I know of a way that's a sure bet you'll sleep well."

She stared, wide-eyed. "Do you?"

He nodded, sagely. "And the way I look at it, you still owe me an apology. I know how we can remedy that, too."

"I…I think you'll have to be a little more clear on what you want."

His gaze never shifted, never faltered.

"You."

She held her breath. And when she finally let it out, his name came out as a whisper.

"Oh…Hale…"

He reached across the table for her hand and covered it with his. His fingers were possessive and strong.

"Is that okay?"

"Yes. It's very okay."

"Sure?"

Diane rolled her eyes. "Cross my heart and hope to die, sure."

Everything after that, until they reached his apartment and almost immediately began to kiss as if they'd been stranded in the desert for days without water, Diane could not recall. It would be a long time before she could remember the street where he lived, whether or not there was a doorman, how many floors there were to the building, what view was beyond the window. Weeks before she actually knew how much space Hale had, since certainly that first night they never got farther than the bedroom.

Diane fell into a delirium of pure sensation, long delayed by time and ill feelings. She and Hale could barely separate long enough to remove their clothes. And she blanked out that woman from the reception. She couldn't have been that important.

There was nothing graceful about the reignition of the flame that stoked their desire for each other. At least, not the first time. There was just an immediate need to quench the thirst. She wanted Hale deep within her, in the most private and personal way. She wanted to lie beneath him, at her most vulnerable, open and submissive, like a sacrifice. Locked together in an intense rhythmic dance until they were both panting and drained. Weak and spent.

Only once they'd taken the edge off with a deeply satisfying release and slow, languid kissing, did they begin again. Taking their time to explore and reclaim and to please each other.

Saying she was sorry never felt so good. She apologized, wholeheartedly. Repeatedly. And Hale accepted…again and again.

He was almost finished dressing when she awoke the next morning.

She stretched like a cat, an unconscious smile curving the corners of her mouth. Rolling onto her back, Diane lay watching Hale through sleepy eyes, her arms thrown back over her head.

He was standing just inside a walk-in closet.

"Did I oversleep?" Diane asked, finally struggling to untangle herself from the sheets.

Hale turned, buttoning his shirt over his broad bare chest. He grinned.

"Morning."

He came to sit on the side of the bed. She was so glad to see that his gaze was warm and kind of lazy.

"Had a good sleep?"

She smiled, groaning deep in her throat for effect. "I had a wonderful sleep."

Hale bent forward to kiss her. It was light but with underlying passion, like he was holding himself back a little.

She curled her toes.

He kissed her once more and got up to return to the closet.

"Where are you going?" she asked, trying to ignore the thought that they'd just had a one-night stand.

"To work. I have a meeting in a few hours. Stay as long as you like. I'll arrange for a car for you."

"I thought…"

He glanced back briefly to her, but was selecting a tie. "What? You thought what?"

She felt vulnerable but in a different way. "That maybe we could spend the day together. At least have breakfast."

He shook his head. "Can't. Not today."

She got out of the bed, clutching the voluminous sheet around her naked body, dragging it on the floor as she went to him.

"Hale, what do you want from me?" she asked quietly.

He looked at her pensively. "I thought I'd made that clear. The question is, what do you want from *me?*"

That took her by surprise.

"I…I just want to be with you. I've never given you a fair chance before. Well…maybe when we were on St. John. That was a very special time."

"It was." He nodded.

She stared at his chest. "I'm sorry I acted so badly, that I treated you so badly."

"Anything else?" he asked.

She was afraid to say too little but more afraid to say too much.

"I missed you. You may not believe this but I think I'm a better person when I'm with you. When it's just the two of us."

"You got it wrong. You're strong, smart, fearless and beautiful."

Diane looked at him, hope oozing out of her pores. Did she seem needy? Pathetic?

"Di," Hale sighed, putting his arms around her. She

embraced him back and the sheet dropped to the floor. "Last night with you put a lot of life back into me. It was every bit as good as being on St. John. But…"

The air went out of her. "You don't…care anymore."

"It's not that I don't care. Far from it. When we make love it's like magic. We are very good together. But I want more. Not just that part of you, but all of you. I don't want to settle for scraps anymore.

"I want what Adam and Eva have."

Chapter 11

She couldn't get Hale's comment out of her mind.

I want what Adam and Eva have.

So did she.

But Diane knew it was not going to be a simple thing of just telling Hale so. Words were not going to be enough. There was first of all the whole matter of letting him know how she felt about him. In her mind and heart the words were there. But trying to get them out of her throat and letting them roll from her tongue seemed insurmountable.

Would Hale believe her?

Diane huddled in the lobby of the science building and was oblivious to the traffic of students and faculty passing through on their way to classes, labs, meetings. She couldn't last much longer in her present state. Confused but determined. Afraid...but determined. How was she to get from what she wanted to actually having it? What could she do to convince Hale that they were perfect for one another? As her father had once said to her, each other's equal. Could she convince Hale that she loved him?

"That bad, huh?"

She looked up at her father. When she was a little girl and spent holidays and summers with him after he and her mother divorced, Diane used to see him as this giant. He could do anything. He was her hero. And she was turning to him now because she needed his guidance and strength to keep her on track or, as he had already told her as well, she was going to blow it.

"Worse," she croaked, trying to keep both panic and tears at bay.

"Let's go get lunch. I'll treat."

"Daddy, I really don't think I could eat a thing."

"Well, I can. I'm hungry. Let's go."

Diane smiled at him as they walked out the exit and into a light rain. But it wasn't cold and there was a real sense that spring wasn't so far away. She couldn't wait. Winter had been filled with far too much drama.

They went to a campus café and Diane had the feeling that the choice of venue was deliberate. Her father, like the students themselves, always complained about the horrible processed food on campus. But the dining hall would be busy and noisy with students and staff, ensuring that no one would be necessarily listening to their conversation and she was less likely to start crying.

Diane was pleased to see that she'd put the fear of God into her father and he was doing better about what he ate when away from home. Tuna salad on whole wheat with a small salad, coffee and a Skinny Cow ice cream bar.

She got a bowl of soup, not wanting to give her stomach any more reason to protest, other than her own emotional state.

"So, talk to me," Adam said, digging into his lunch with gusto.

Diane didn't want to whine. And she knew that her father, maybe more than anyone, understood what she'd been going through and how she'd gotten there. He'd always said that the two of them were alike.

She was honest with her father, open with him, within reason, about her relationship with Hale. And Adam didn't need all the facts, the blow-by-blow. He got the picture.

"Do you think he's in love with you?"

She shook her head. "I don't know. He gives all the signs sometimes. Does all the right things. But I feel like Hale is holding back."

"You mean, like you?"

Diane frowned at her father.

"You know, when your mother and I divorced I was like a raging bull. It was an ugly divorce, Diane. And I stayed ugly for a long time after. I was angry and disappointed. I was never going to go through that again. Hurt too much. Tore my gut out. It seemed like, when you're in love you're always insecure. I didn't want to be that insecure ever again.

"But, what are the options? You become a robot and dead from the neck down? Meeting Eva put me through the wringer. She didn't know it, of course, but she was so straightforward and a beautiful, good woman. And a whole lot stronger than she seems."

"She had to be, to put up with you."

Adam burst out into a deep, appreciative laugh. He shook his head.

"Yeah, well…look. Love is a choice. Once you make up your mind about who you love you have to work on it. It's not going to happen by itself. You have to step off the edge of the cliff because your heart tells you to, and if you're right about the other person, they will be there to catch you.

"I figured that out when I met Eva that summer on St. John. I'd made a vow that I wasn't going to fall in love with her. But then her vacation ended and she went back home without telling me. And that's when I *really* got scared. I didn't want to lose her. I didn't want to think about what my life would be like without her. I made a vow to myself on St. John that I would go after Eva and convince her how much she means to me. I wanted to spend the rest of my life never letting her forget."

Diane tried to not let her father see that, despite his plans, tears were somehow leaking out of her eyes. She took her napkin and hastily dabbed. She gave her father a watery smile.

"Eva's so lucky."

"*I'm* very lucky."

"Okay, I get it. Daddy, I need you to help me. I need a favor."

"Anything, baby."

"I have to get back to St. John."

When Hale stepped off the ferry he took a moment to dig out his rental car reservation. Adam had made all the arrangements and an agency rep was going to meet him to take him to the car depot. He'd offered to stay at a hotel or even on the sloop until business was concluded, but Adam had insisted that he stay at the house.

Hale grabbed the handle of his weekend leather duffel

and began walking toward Cruz Bay. He'd stuffed his leather jacket inside, only needed for the trip from his apartment to the airport in D.C. It was a relief to be back in warm sunny weather. And despite his doubts that he wasn't really needed on-site to handle Adam's concerns, he was glad to be back.

There weren't that many people who'd disembarked with him, nor were there many waiting at the end of the dock. But one person stood out immediately. He literally stopped in his tracks when he recognized the beautiful slender woman in capri pants and a sleeveless linen blouse, in sandals and a baseball cap with Skinny Legs, the name of a local café, stitched above the brim. Her satisfied smile broadened as he finally continued his approach.

"Hi," Diane said brightly. "Welcome back."

"Hello yourself," Hale responded.

He was sorry he couldn't have been more original or more off-the-cuff, but he was stunned and trying to get his brain around the fact that she was really here. Even more surprising was the light welcome kiss she pressed briefly to his mouth.

"Is that everything?" she asked, pointing to his duffel.

"And this," Hale said, patting his computer case hanging from his shoulder.

"I have a Jeep over here," Diane said, walking confidently toward the small parking lot and a rented Wrangler.

"You father arranged for…"

"I know. I canceled it. Put your things in the back."

Hale was beginning to feel as if he'd fallen down the rabbit hole. It was a free-fall ride and he knew he'd have to give in to it and figure it all out when he hit bottom. He just prayed that the velocity didn't kill him.

But for the moment he grappled with confusion, suspicion and an overwhelming happiness that swelled within him because Diane was next to him, in an open Jeep, on St. John. Just the two of them. Alone together.

She pulled out her GPS, silently and expertly mounting it on the dashboard. Hale laughed lightly.

"What's so funny? You should be glad I'm using it."

"I think it's funny that you still don't know how to get to the house."

"Who said I didn't?" Diane asked coyly.

He looked at her profile as she backed out of the space, shifting gears with much more finesse and ease since he'd first taught her. He continued to watch her, pleased by her presence, her beauty and the woman she had now become, even since the holidays. He had no desire for Diane to lose her dauntless spirit, her willfulness, but he needed to see it tempered by respect and consideration for him.

"Daddy told me you were coming down."

"Interesting. He didn't tell me you were going to be here."

"I guess he wanted you to be surprised." She shrugged.

"I am." Hale nodded with amusement. "So, why are you here?"

He instantly saw that she hesitated.

"I…had some time. Besides my own work I've been keeping on top of Eva's recovery and a few of Ron's shelter cases. I leave in just three weeks for Africa, and I have a symposium to prepare for."

"Wow. It's a wonder you have time for anything else."

She gave him a quick calm glance. "I make time for the things that are important to me."

Hale thought about that. He couldn't help wondering what else was on the list. "So you're going to be busy."

"So will you," she answered quickly. "We'll probably have no time to really see each other. Daddy said he's asked you to take care of some legal issue for him."

"Yes, he did," Hale said. "But as long as I'm here I intend to make the most of it."

He noticed how skilled a driver she'd become as Diane tore up the incline in second gear from the main road to the flat parking area just below the house. Hale chuckled to himself at the way she attacked life. She held nothing back. He hoped that was true in other ways. Already he was distracted from the purpose of his return to the island. Already he was considering the possibilities and his own desires. He thought he'd be alone for the four days he'd committed to on Adam's behalf. Now that he knew Diane was also going to be staying at the house, it was either going to be much too long or much too short a time.

She silently led the way up to the veranda. It was clear to Hale that she had been there at least since the day before, since there were only two flights a day in and out of St. Thomas. Her own computer case was on the floor and her laptop on the dining table. There were folders and books next to it and a used cup that probably had contained coffee or tea earlier.

Diane took off her cap, dropped it on a chair and stood, legs akimbo, fluffing her flattened hair and combing it with her fingers. The motion caused her blouse to press against her body and Hale could detect that she wore no bra. Her nipples left tiny round protrusions in the front.

The telltale signs in his body of arousal betrayed him, and he quickly turned to the stairs leading to the upper level.

"I guess I'm staying up here?" He was already climbing the flight.

"If you want," Diane said softly behind him.

He stopped, turned back to look down at her.

"I have a choice?"

"You always have a choice," she said quietly.

He reversed his steps and dropped the bag on the floor. It landed with a thud.

"And where are you sleeping?"

She pointed blindly. "On the terrace where I stayed at Christmas. I like it there."

"What do you think I should do?"

Her expression grew pensive and she stared thoughtfully at him. "The last time we were together you said we should take one step at a time. It didn't seem very encouraging when you said it, but I think you're right. Let's not plan anything, Hale. You're here for a reason. I have work to do, myself. And we're here together. When things happen, hopefully it will be the way they're supposed to happen."

He had to admire her strength of purpose. And he realized it was a very sensible idea. He knew they were both teetering on the brink of something. One false move could end it all. He didn't want that to happen. He wasn't expecting this, but he realized his whole future hung in the balance

"Fair enough. We'll let instincts rule."

"Fair enough." She turned away and headed into the kitchen. "What are your plans for this afternoon?"

Hale stayed where he was, listening to glasses being put on the counter, to something being poured. To the refrigerator door opening and closing. She stepped back into the space and handed him a glass. It was guava juice. He'd first had it here on St. John and loved it. He accepted the glass and raised it slightly in salute to her. Somehow she'd known.

"Not much left to the afternoon. I'm going to make a few calls to let the local authorities know I'm on the island. I have a couple of meetings tomorrow. Other things might come up. And you?"

"Back to my computer. I'm finishing up a basic outline for my symposium presentation. It's going to be a PowerPoint so I have to think about my visuals. Dinner is at seven, is that okay?"

"You cooking?"

"Unless you want to."

"Seven is fine."

Hale retrieved his bag and climbed to the upper level where there were two rooms. Both were of equal size, and both were comfortably appointed. He chose the one facing out over the water, almost above where Diane would be sleeping.

He unpacked and tried to review his plans for the next few days. They pertained to Adam's desire to buy an adjoining lot of land and to possibly build on it in the future. Hale needed to find out about access rights, since another road might need to be cleared at some point. There were also water rights and a plan for ecological building for the least damage to the land. This was not his area of expertise by any stretch of the imagination.

But Adam trusted him and he was going to make sure he got it right.

That Diane was also going to be around definitely put a monkey wrench in his plans to use his extra time to think about his future. But the truth was, a lot of that was about her.

He'd come so close once to telling her openly he loved her. He'd known it for a very long time. But what happened when they were leaving St. John after Christmas had knocked the wind out of him and he was afraid to reveal the depth of his desire. He wasn't sure what he would do if Diane threw his declaration back in his face.

But then there was that night at his apartment. She'd been so passionate, so...loving, confirming yet again for him how perfectly they fit. How well they read one another's needs. At least to the extent that it happened in bed. She'd admitted she wanted to be with him. He believed her. But he was equally as committed to what he wanted. The whole nine yards. All or nothing. He was never going to accept half measure again.

Hale had a suspicion that there was far more to the story of Diane coincidentally being on St. John the same time as himself. He was a lawyer. And he'd survived a long time on his street smarts before meeting Adam Maxwell. He didn't believe in coincidence.

He changed clothes and went back down to sit in the living room, his notes and papers and laptop spread over the coffee table. Less than ten feet away Diane was at work on her own business and didn't even acknowledge his return. Only for a short time did it feel awkward to be in the same room with her, ignoring her as she did her thing and he did his. But they did.

To his surprise Hale became totally immersed in his

work, trying to get a handle on something he wasn't very familiar with. He didn't notice her turn on the lights as it grew dark. Didn't realize the quiet music was from the satellite station on the radio. Didn't pay much attention to Diane in the kitchen until incredible smells began to waft into the living room where he worked. Without being prompted, Hale closed his computer and got up to set the table for dinner.

Slowly, conversation came into play. Commonplace topics and things having to do with the next few days. Questions about the property and his answers, her opinions. Questions about her symposium and her answers.

Dinner was simple. Broiled fish, with island rice and beans, crusty rolls she'd actually made and wine.

"I guess you were surprised to see me," she suddenly said, as they sat after dinner enjoying a second glass of wine.

"You could say that."

"Are you sorry I'm here?"

He stared at her. "Are you fishing?"

"Yes."

"No, I'm not."

"Then, I have something else to ask…."

He shook his head. "You don't have to. The woman at the reception is a friend. A colleague. She's married, and I don't do married women, okay?"

She nodded.

She seemed to relax and Hale suddenly realized that, for all his uncertainty, Diane was in no better shape. He took heart and hope in that.

They cleared away dinner, cleaned and closed down the kitchen. She went off to take a shower, he took a last look at his papers and then decided he'd done enough for the night. The distraction of work had...stopped working.

Diane had the nerve to come out of the bathroom wrapped in nothing but a towel. It was nearly his undoing, and he knew she was playing with him. *Well, two can play that game*, he muttered in his head.

"I'm going to bed. What time is your first meeting tomorrow?"

"About nine-thirty," he said, realizing there was a distinct gravelly pitch to his voice.

"Okay, I'll be ready to drive you down to Cruz Bay. Good night. Sleep tight."

He said nothing, just watched as she sashayed toward her alcove.

"You forgot something," Hale found himself saying.

She glanced over a bare shoulder and raised her brows.

He waited.

She shook her head.

He started walking silently toward her. She was waiting, anticipating his move.

Witch! Hale thought caustically to himself. She was going to try and make him beg.

Not in this lifetime.

But now was not the time to quibble over details. She was already lifting her face to him, opening her mouth. He captured her lips, manipulating until they opened to his satisfaction and he could slip his tongue in. It was incredibly hot, the whole day building up as one big tease. He didn't care just then. He kissed her the way he'd wanted to since seeing her on the pier that afternoon. But he didn't touch her. He let the slow rocking of his mouth against hers say what he couldn't.

And he took her ready response as encouragement that neither of them should give up.

Hale broke the kiss and could sense her reluctance for it to end. He had grown hard the minute their lips touched.

But a man has his pride!

"Good night," he whispered seductively, and turned away from her.

Hale waited until Diane had gone to bed and turned out her light. He got himself another glass of wine, brooding over the cat-and-mouse game he suspected they were playing. It was hard to tell who had the upper hand for the moment, but as it got late and he finally went to his room, he sort of knew it wasn't him.

It was around two in the morning when he thought he'd held out long enough. No one could blame him, he thought, if he sought comfort in the arms of someone who wanted him. Someone he wanted, *badly*. He had had a full erection since the kiss and knew if he didn't do something about it, it was going to be a very long night. In which case, he wanted only to do it with her.

He climbed out of bed and silently walked down a level, through the kitchen, and stood in the doorway of her room. His eyes adjusted to the dark and he could see Diane had a sheet lightly covering her. She was still and he thought her asleep. But suddenly, she slowly pushed aside the sheet and Hale caught his breath and grew even harder when he saw that she was naked, as was he.

She said not a word, but held up her arms and he approached, climbing into the invitation.

He wanted her so bad his head throbbed, as did another prominent part of him. She reached low between his legs to stroke him, aware of his great need, as if trying to ease his ache. He rocked against her soft gentle hands, dizzy with desire. But he pushed her hand away and shifted position. There was something else he needed to do first, for her. It was his way of thanking Diane for not giving up on him. On the possibility of *them*.

"Yes," she moaned, opening her legs as his shoulders slid beneath her knees.

Hale stroked her thighs as his lips kissed her nether part. She moaned again and raised her hips to meet him, while his tongue delicately searched for the ways that made her feel good.

"Hale...oh, my God. Oooooh," Diane panted.

But just as he sensed she was going to come Hale crawled back up her body and buried himself in her, in one smooth thrust of his hips. The ride was a short one, but it ended with both of them clutching each other, twisting together, moaning in the sweet agony of release.

Diane held his head to her, stroking his head and shoulders. He loved the soft cushion of her breasts and the slender cradle of her legs about him. For a very long time, until he was almost asleep, he was content just where he was.

"I guess I should go back upstairs."

"Only if you want to."

"Tomorrow is going to be a long day. I'm not going to be much good if I don't get some sleep."

She kissed his forehead. "So, go to sleep."

Hale's body gave in and he did.

Diane waded through the shallow surf to the shore, sluicing the water from her hair with her hands and feeling the last of the late afternoon sun beginning to warm her chilled skin. Dripping water, she trudged

up the beach slope to her towel and sat down wearily.
Hale would have a fit if he knew she'd gone swimming
without him or someone else with her, at least on the
beach, to spot her as she swam almost out to the opening
of the bay and back again.

But she had to do something to cool her ragged
nerves. She realized that they were both once again
leaving the next morning and there had been no word
between them about the future.

What was he waiting for?

Diane groaned as she fell back on the towel with her
eyes closed.

What was she going to do?

That first night together had been so right. So natural.
Spending it squeezed together on the too-small double
daybed, she'd thought it was a promising beginning.
And it had been. They hadn't slept apart since arriving,
and she'd looked forward to every evening because she
knew that, in each other's arms, they were going to find
bliss, mutual satisfaction and peace. Diane recognized
that it had gone far beyond the physical for her, but she'd
known that back in D.C. Her feelings had tipped over
the edge into the full-blown realm of love.

And it seemed to be killing her.

As perfect as they were together in bed, she'd come
to see that their compatibility went much further. There
was a give-and-take between them that now was in sync
and comfortable. They could communicate in shorthand,
sometimes just with a look, a simple word or phrase.
They tested and challenged each other, neither ever
backing down, and she was thrilled that Hale was not
the least bit intimidated by her, nor would he let her get
over on him. Except for the business of how she came

to be on St. John at exactly the same time as he. If he questioned it, he kept it to himself.

But that's as far as it went. And she was frustrated. They were running out of time, and she was deathly afraid that the four days they were secluded together had been nothing more than an enjoyable tryst for him. It had become so much more for her.

Simply put, she didn't want to lose him. And she was scared. What if he didn't love her? What if she'd really ruined any chance of that by her outrageous behavior over the years?

Realizing that she wasn't going to find the answer sitting on the beach, Diane checked the time on her cell phone and began to put on her clothes over her still-wet suit. She needed to get started back to the house, and it was going to be all uphill, following a well-worn path that she had been using since she was a child and first came to the island.

She was in the shower when Hale returned. He knocked on the door and told her to put on something pretty and cool. He was taking her out to dinner.

She put on her happy face and cheerful demeanor, determined that no matter what, Hale would never know that he alone, of any man she'd ever known, had been the one able to break her heart.

It helped that he held her hand all evening and spoke easily, with great satisfaction, about how he believed he'd accomplished what Adam had sent him to do. It helped that he told her how beautiful she was…and that the past three days with her had been incredible. It helped that he admitted he wished they had more time.

When they went to bed that night she believed it was for the last time. She didn't think she had the strength to continue to see Hale back in D.C. knowing how she felt, what she wanted. She'd make up a story for her parents, she'd take all the blame if she had to, do what she needed to, to move on.

Again.

Alone.

She did welcome their lovemaking, the old-fashioned way. She loved the feel of him on top of her, his weight protecting her. She loved the play of his muscles as his flanks and thighs and buttocks and stomach flexed and contracted as he thrust into her. She was glad she didn't have to ask Hale to slow down, take his time to make it last. He seemed to know to kiss her slowly and deeply, to be tender.

When she came she cried. Silently so that Hale could not see. She made her own vow that he would not know she could never love anyone as much as she loved him.

Now was not the time to pretend otherwise.

The airport was as crowded as always. She'd never made a trip down or back when the waiting area wasn't filled with tired, sunburned, post-vacation families and couples returning to the mainland. Hale managed to find them two seats opposite one another while they waited for the boarding announcement for their flight. It infuriated Diane that Hale sat reading legal briefs while her stomach roiled and protested and her misery grew.

One flight was announced and a dozen people in their sector gathered their bags and headed for the departure gate. Diane shifted seats so they could sit together.

She couldn't stand it anymore.

"Aren't you going to say *anything*?" she asked suddenly, her anxiety infusing her voice with a sharp tone.

Hale looked at her, puzzled. "About what?"

"Hale!" she nearly shrieked. "How can you ask that? About us! About being together on St. John. About going back home."

She'd held her nervousness in so long, she realized she was breathing hard.

"I loved being on the island with you. I'm not looking forward to going back to D.C."

"Well!"

"Well...what?"

She stood up. "You're doing this on purpose. You're trying to make me mad."

He stood up as well. "You're doing a good job of that all by yourself," Hale said calmly. "Just what is your problem?"

"It's not *my* problem, it's *our* problem."

"Sorry. I don't see it that way. Until you tell me what this is about, it's all yours."

Diane could hardly breathe again. Her chest felt tight. Her heart was racing. She thought she wanted to hit him.

No.

She wanted to fall into his arms and...and...

"How can you say that to me? The last few months, when we've been together, I..."

"Yes?"

"Well, I thought you and I..."

"Di," he said seriously, taking a step closer to her, his brows furrowed. "See, that's the thing. You were thinking more about your feelings and not much about me at all."

She gasped. "That's not true! At Christmas..."

"Let's not forget how that ended. You jumped to conclusions...just like you're about to do now."

She swallowed, momentarily chastened. "Okay, I admit I was an idiot at Christmas. I've tried to apologize and show you I...I've changed. This is different. I know it is."

He nodded. "Okay. How is it different?"

"Because it is," Diane said impatiently, waving her arms. Several people got up around them and quietly changed their seats.

"You'll have to do better than that," Hale said flatly.

She realized he was not going to give an inch.

"You're just trying to get back at me for...for what happened. Because I..."

"I'm listening."

She gasped. Against her will, inexplicably, a quiet sob escaped. Her eyes pleaded with him as her will began to give out.

"I didn't give you a chance. And if I had, maybe you would have...some feelings for me."

"Is that what you want from me? Feelings?"

"What I want is...Hale, don't you care for me at all? Even a little?"

He stepped even closer. His gaze narrowed on her. Her chest heaved as she gazed into his face, looking for some softening or a hint of understanding.

"Why don't we do this, Di. You tell me how you feel. Take a chance, the same way you expected me to. Don't play with it. Don't try to work it or get over. Just do it. For just this once, say what *you* really feel. Tell me what *you* want. Don't you remember what I said to you the night of Eva's surgery?"

His voice had gotten hard again. But she knew it wasn't because he was angry. It was because he wasn't going to let her get away with putting it all on him.

"Hale...I'm...scared."

"You're not afraid of anything."

She looked at him and lost the battle. Her eyes brimmed over. And as if he'd just challenged her, Diane raised her quivering chin and stood determined.

"I love you. I'm *so* in love with you, I think it hurts."

"What? What did you say?" He leaned down to her.

"Damn you, Hale. I said I love you. And if you don't care, fine. I'll get over it."

"Diane..."

"The last few days have been so beautiful I was so sure you felt the same way I do."

"I do."

"And I waited for you to say something and you didn't."

"I just did."

"So now I've made a fool of myself, in front of all these people who probably feel sorry for me."

"They probably feel sorry for me," Hale corrected.

There was noticeable laughter from those close enough to hear their exchange.

"I can't help the way I feel about you, Di. It sure didn't happen right away. I've cared about you for a long time. You made me wait a very long time to say I love you."

Diane swallowed and her eyes brightened. "Does that mean..." She stopped, wanting him to fill in the blank.

"What should it mean?"

He was relentless, and she loved him all the more for making her say it out loud.

She hesitated and suddenly frowned. "Did you just say you loved me?"

"Yes," Hale said simply.

She stared with her mouth gaping at him, as if she couldn't believe it or expected him to vanish in a puff of smoke. Diane gave an enormous, ear-piercing scream and propelled herself clear off the floor into Hale's arms, wrapping her legs around his waist.

"Will you marry me, Hale Cameron?" she asked, the question muffled and lost in his neck as she hugged him. Held on to him as though her life depended on it.

"Thank God! Enough, already," someone groused in the crowd of witnesses. People laughed.

Diane never let go of her hold around Hale's neck, but she loosened her leg wrap and put her feet back on the floor.

"You mean it?" Diane asked, staring at him, knowing her own love was written all over her face.

"I better. I'm tired of fighting. I just want to love you."

"Hale...me, too," Diane said, her voice thin and high.

She was glad when he finally stopped her from talking and just kissed her, much to the entertainment of the entire airport waiting room, who whistled and wolfed them.

It was the best medicine for what had ailed both of them.

Chapter 12

"It's really going to happen," Diane murmured, staring at her reflection in the mirror.

Behind her Eva chuckled. She was slightly bent over as she carefully attached one more flower to the colorful arrangement pinned to her hair.

"Are you excited? You and I have hardly had any time to talk since you told Adam and me that you were getting married."

"Excited?" Diane repeated. "It took an awful long time to get here. I'm very happy. And I finally feel quiet inside. Does that make sense?"

Eva stood, barely able to see over the top of Diane's head as Diane sat in front of the vanity. She cupped her shoulders and squeezed.

"Honey, it makes perfect sense. Everything does when you're in love. What do you think?"

Diane turned her head slowly left and right, and then smiled. "It's beautiful. Just what I wanted."

"Come on, we have to hurry. I think Simon is waiting with the car to drive you to the pier. You need to be on board before Hale gets there, and the guests."

Diane stood and let her white dress fall and drape gracefully around her slender body. She again turned this way and that.

"You look beautiful," Eva told her.

"Maybe it's too simple. Maybe I should have…"

"You picked the dress that's comfortable for you, and I really think it's a great choice. The wide boat neckline really shows your long neck and face and hair. And I like that the dress isn't fussy."

"Me, too." Diane sighed, reassured.

"Where's your mother?" Eva asked placidly, her back turned to Diane as she bent to pick up her purse from an ottoman.

"Probably outside complaining about anything and everything. You know if it's not her way it's wrong."

"I'm sorry, honey but don't let it upset you. Especially not today."

"I won't. Believe me, I know my mother and how to say no to her. She's really a smart, beautiful woman. But she requires a lot of patience." Diane faced the mirror again. "Am I missing anything?"

"Just this."

Eva approached her and reached up her arms to Diane. Diane had to bend over to accommodate her stepmother's petite height, but they hugged one another with great affection and warmth.

"I'm so happy for you and Hale. Your father and I believed for years that you two would be good for each other."

"I wish I'd seen it sooner. Think of all that time we lost because of me."

"Things happen when they're supposed to happen. You know, after my husband and daughter were killed you could not have convinced me that I'd ever marry again. When I came down to St. John for that vacation Adam was the last person I was looking to meet. And he didn't make it easy to love him."

"I know. He told me. He said he was scared. So was I, Eva. I wanted a perfect relationship, a perfect marriage like you and Daddy."

Eva laughed merrily. "Forget that. Ain't no such thing as perfect. You have to work on it every day. Your father and I, we've been blessed, it's true."

"That's what I want, Eva. I want Hale and I to look at each other twenty, thirty years from now and still feel the same way."

Eva looked at her watch. "Well, those twenty or thirty years are due to start in about an hour. Let's go."

Diane and Hale wanted to break all the rules. And they did.

They first agreed that they wanted their wedding, admittedly the second for both of them, to be memorably different. There was instant agreement that the wedding would be held on St. John. They eschewed tradition and decided that everyone, family and friends alike, should wear white.

They took an additional risk and planned the event at the end of July, before the known start of hurricane season in the Caribbean. There was a very short window of opportunity and they decided to go for it.

The ceremony was going to be aboard the *Paradise*, and Adam had arranged for two locals to crew the sloop so that he would not have to. A route had been charted along the Windward Passage to The Narrows and Great Thatch Island, where it would turn and make the journey back. The single-mast sloop could only legally carry a small number of passengers when under sail, so the ceremony guests were pretty much immediate family.

Diane and Eva were helped into the Jeep by Simon. He was dressed in white linen pants and a short-sleeved white shirt as, it turned out, would nearly all of the men that day. They drove down to the marina to take the first skiff ride out to the *Paradise*. Word had quickly spread, as it is wont to do on a small island, that there was going to be a wedding. Everyone knew Adam and Eva Maxwell. And just by their presence they honored the marriage of his daughter, Diane, whom many had known since she was a small girl coming down for vacations and school break.

Anchored just beyond the shore, the *Paradise* stood out with its lines, railings and trim decorated with white flowing streams of ribbons and flowers and balloons. Hayden and Bailey were already waiting, as were Diane's mother, Maron, and her stepfather. One of the hired ship crew ferried them to the sloop.

Diane was relieved to see that the local minister, a middle-aged woman originally from St. Croix, was to perform the ceremony. Wood instruments do not fair well in sea air, and the decision was made to use a trio of horns for the music on board. Nautical law also forbade any furniture that was not secured to the vessel, so plush cushions were provided so that guests could sit wherever there was a space.

In a few hours the *Paradise* would dock again and the wedding dinner would take place at the Turtle Bay Estate House at Caneel. She and Hale knew that Ron had come down. Another added surprise was Jenna and Colby, her husband, whom Diane had yet to meet as he'd returned from overseas just a month earlier.

Diane went below for one last look at herself. Her stomach was beginning to flutter. She wanted to marry Hale more than anything but she was nervous.

She admitted to herself that having Hale as her husband meant everything to her. Together they could create their own lives, future and happiness. She wanted to do it right this time. It could not be about her, but about them.

There was a quiet knock on the below cabin door. She thought it was Eva or Bailey or someone letting her know it was time. But she didn't have a chance to open the door or even to answer. It quickly opened and Hale slipped inside.

She gasped. "What are you doing here? You're not supposed to see me yet. The ceremony is going…"

That's as far as she got before Hale gathered her in his arms and embraced and kissed her. Complaints died in her throat. Her arms slipped around his neck and she leaned into him.

"Hale…" she whispered when she could talk.

"We're making up our own rules, remember? This is our party. I wanted to kiss you. Period."

"Yes." She nodded, angling her mouth toward his again.

They were well into a satisfying foray of lips and tongues when there was another knock.

"Hale, are you in there?"

"I love you," Hale whispered against her lips. "Yeah. Coming," he said louder, blowing her one more kiss and ducking out the door again.

She stood grinning, ear to ear, touching her fingers to her mouth.

The flutters stopped.

Bailey was the maid of honor, eliminating any disappointment from her mother or Eva that they would be matron of honor. They were both okay with the break in tradition. But there was no question that Adam was to be Hale's best man. Hale decided that Eva would be the flower girl and Maron would carry the wedding bands.

Diane and Hale wrote their own vows.

They were under sail when the horns began to play, in royal blasts, the wedding march. It was a picture-perfect day, the air clean and clear, a slight sea breeze bellowing the sails and carrying the sounds of the music across the water. Boaters up and down the passage shouted and waved or blew their horns.

Diane thought she might cry, and Hale looked mesmerized and emotional. He absorbed the minister's prayers and their shared scripted vows. Hale spoke first.

"I, Hale, come here today to join my life to yours before our family and friends. You are all I could ever want in my life. I promise to be faithful to you, to love you, honor you and cherish you. This is my solemn vow."

And then it was Diane's turn.

"I, Diane…Di…promise to give you the best of myself. I promise to accept you the way you are. I promise to keep myself open to you. Life has given us a second chance at happiness. I vow that this will be my only love, from this day forward."

Diane could see in Hale's eyes that he meant to honor

his vows. And when they were announced man and wife everything and everyone around them faded away and, in their first kiss as a blessed couple, she believed with her whole heart that they both felt the same thing.

They had found paradise in each other.

"Does anyone know where we are?" Diane asked in a lazy, sated voice.

Hale kissed the top of her head. "Nope. Adam and Eva swore their lips were sealed. It was pretty generous of that couple who own the chain of stores on Puerto Rico to let us honeymoon in their guesthouse."

"Some guesthouse." She sighed, in her mind recounting the six bedrooms and as many baths, an outdoor disappearing pool, an indoor and outdoor dining area, a kitchen as large as one of the bedrooms. They'd even been given the services of a cook, which was a good thing. They had far better things to do with their time. Most of it was spent alone together in the master suite, with its sweeping panoramic view of the Caribbean Sea. But the best part was the isolation. High atop a hill overlooking Francis and Cinnamon Bay, where during the day they could see a dozen islands dotting the sea and a true horizon beyond.

Diane shifted and Hale accommodated her so that she could get comfortable and snuggle against him. They were lounging together on a Balinese daybed, the huge square structure with its thick covered mattress and at least a dozen large pillows was set up on the terrace next to the pool. They had turned out all of the outdoor lights and lit hurricane lamps all around the terrace. It made the space exotic and romantic.

Hale was more or less stretched out, reclining on some of those pillows, while Diane lay atop him, her back to his chest. He cradled her with his arm around her.

"I could stay like this forever."

"No. I don't think so. Sooner or later I want to go home."

"Home." She turned her head on his chest to grin at him "Our home."

Hale remained silent but smiled at her as he stroked her arm. "Are you disappointed we didn't plan a real honeymoon?"

"This is a real honeymoon together. You mean that we didn't do a trip or something? No. I don't miss it. As long as I can be with you it's a honeymoon."

"Very nice, Mrs. Cameron."

"Thank you, Mr. Cameron."

She began kissing his chest, little butterfly touches of her lips. He began to grow hard beneath her, the length of him pulsing.

"Do you think there's such a thing as dying from too much love?" Hale asked, his voice suddenly rich and deeper with growing desire.

She giggled, turning over to lick a nipple and wiggle her hips seductively against his. "Well...there was Romeo and Juliet."

He put his hands on either side of her head, tilting her face so that he could kiss her. "Yeah. I heard about them. Kids."

She began to laugh, his comment so funny and so true. Hale took the opportunity to gently flip her onto her back, kissing down her neck and chest, his hand caressing and kneading her breasts, making its way to her mons veneris, and further. Her laugh caught in her throat and became a soft, drawn-out moan. She lay submissive, delirious.

"Hale...I...I'm so glad...you love me."

He removed his hand and replaced it with another, more fitting part of his anatomy. She welcomed him.

"Forever," he whispered, quickly bringing them both to a state of utter delight. "I promise."

* * * * *

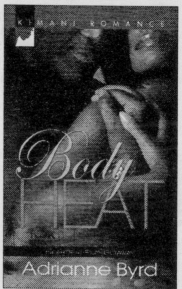

*Is this their siren
song of love?*

TEMPTATION'S
Song

JANICE
SIMS

For talented singer Elle Jones, going to Italy was supposed to be a
vacation. Instead, she's been cast in Dominic Corelli's next opera.
The relentlessly driven director arouses desire like nothing Elle has
ever known. She knows she's playing with fire, but can she resist
Dominic's melody of seduction?

> "Sims again displays her gift for using unusual situations
> and settings, larger-than-life characters, a drop of humor
> and a feel-good romance to tell a story."
> —*RT Book Reviews* on *That Summer at American Beach*

*Coming the first week of July 2010
wherever books are sold.*

REQUEST YOUR FREE BOOKS!

2 FREE NOVELS PLUS 2 FREE GIFTS!

KIMANI™ ROMANCE

Love's ultimate destination!

KROM10R

L♥VE IN THE LIMELIGHT

Fantasy, Fame and Fortune...Hollywood-Style!

Book #1
By *New York Times* and *USA TODAY*
Bestselling Author Brenda Jackson

STAR OF HIS HEART
August 2010

Book #2
By A.C. Arthur

SING YOUR PLEASURE
September 2010

Book #3
By Ann Christopher

SEDUCED ON THE RED CARPET
October 2010

Book #4
By *Essence* Bestselling Author Adrianne Byrd

LOVERS PREMIERE
November 2010

*Set in Hollywood's entertainment industry,
two unstoppable sisters and their two friends
find romance, glamour and dreams-come-true.*

KIMANI™
ROMANCE

www.kimanipress.com
www.myspace.com/kimanipress

KPLITLSP